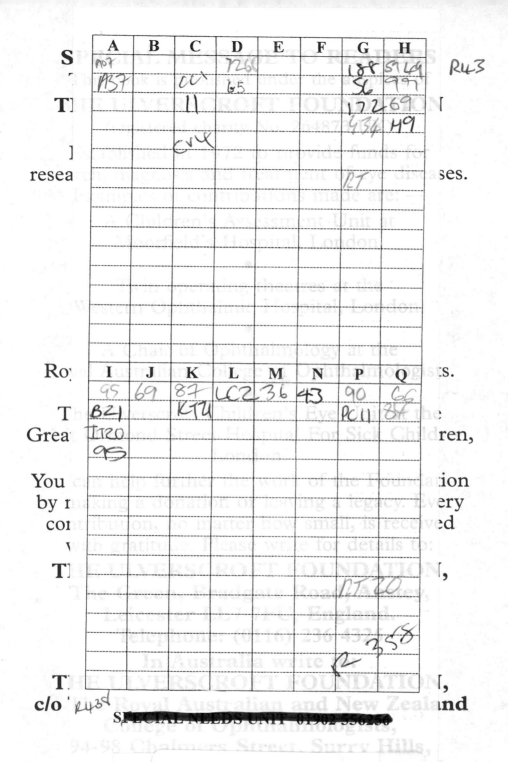

Marina Oliver has published almost fifty novels under various pseudonyms, plus half a dozen non-fiction books. She has written historical novels as well as twentieth-century sagas, contemporary romances and crime. Marina has been the Chairman of the Romantic Novelists' Association and has also edited various magazines and novels. She now splits her time between rural Shropshire and Madeira and is married with four children and several grandchildren.

For more details on the author visit Marina's website:
www.marina-oliver.net/

GRETNA LEGACY

Abigail Barton was brought up in Bath by
Lady Jordan; her own parents died when
she was a baby. Now her trustee, Mr
Wood, insists that she goes to London for
the Season, but Abby has no desire to
marry. Abigail's sponsor, Lady Padmore, is
bringing out her own daughter, Caroline,
this Season, determined to marry her to
cousin Julian. Meanwhile, Julian, intrigued
by Abigail's unconventionality, lends his
house for the ball. Then Abby's childhood
friend, Hartley, arrives in London, Caroline's brother Dudley sells out from the
army, and among the offers of marriage,
she must accept someone — but whom?

Books by Marina Oliver
Published by The House of Ulverscroft:

HIGHLAND DESTINY
CAVALIER COURTSHIP
LORD HUGO'S BRIDE
THE BARON'S BRIDE
RUNAWAY HILL
MASQUERADE FOR THE KING
LORD HUGO'S WEDDING
CAMPAIGN FOR A BRIDE
RESTORATION AFFAIR
COURTESAN OF THE SAINTS
THE ACCIDENTAL MARRIAGE
A DISGRACEFUL AFFAIR
SUPERVISING SALLY
SCANDAL AT THE DOWER HOUSE

MARINA OLIVER

◆

GRETNA LEGACY

Complete and Unabridged

ULVERSCROFT
Leicester

First published in Great Britain in 2010 by
Robert Hale Limited
London

First Large Print Edition
published 2011
by arrangement with
Robert Hale Limited
London

British Library CIP Data

Oliver, Marina, *1934 –*
  Gretna legacy.
  1. London (England)- -Social life and customs- -
  Fiction. 2. Love stories. 3. Large type books.
  I. Title
  823.9'14–dc22

  ISBN 978–1–4448–0709–7

Published by
F. A. Thorpe (Publishing)
Anstey, Leicestershire

Set by Words & Graphics Ltd.
Anstey, Leicestershire
Printed and bound in Great Britain by
T. J. International Ltd., Padstow, Cornwall

This book is printed on acid-free paper

1

Abigail Barton held up her skimpy skirts with an exaggerated twist of her hands, skipped two steps to the right, then two to the left, keeping her nose raised and her gaze on the grey clouds above Pulteney Bridge. When she collided with a solid male body and found strong arms supporting her she emitted an 'ooff' of surprise and lowered her gaze.

'Oh, it's you, Hartley. Why can't you keep out of my way?'

The young man she spoke to removed the arms he had flung around her and gave her an exaggerated bow. He was tall and broad, blond and handsome, dressed in pale biscuit pantaloons and an excellently tailored blue superfine coat.

'What the devil were you doing, brat, prancing about like that?'

She curtsied. 'La, kind sir, that wasn't prancing. I've just been to my dancing lesson, I was practising.'

'Dancing? Don't you know all the steps?'

She sighed, abandoning her pose. 'Yes, but Aunt Emily insists. Dancing on Monday, singing on Tuesday, the pianoforte on

1

Wednesday, drawing and water colours on Thursday and, until I flatly refused to go any more, the harp on Friday. It's all part of her campaign to make me an accomplished young lady.'

'She's wasting her time,' he said, chuckling.

'Thank you, Hartley dear! I assume you mean I'm already marvellously accomplished?'

'I wouldn't dare suggest otherwise.'

'She's trying to think of something else to keep me occupied, but when I suggested fencing she threw up her hands in horror. Really, you'd think I was ten years old instead of eighteen.'

'Don't you want to have all the accomplishments of a young lady when you go to London?'

'No, Hartley, I don't want to go to London! I don't know this woman my trustees have inveigled into presenting me. Just because her husband was an old friend of Mr Wood's doesn't mean I'll like her, or her precious Caroline. Why can't Aunt Emily take me to London?'

Hartley Lennox grinned at her. 'How often has Lady Jordan been to London in the past twenty years? How many of the *ton* does she know?'

Abby sighed. 'Yes, but that's not important.

I don't want to be presented, and meet all those wretched *ton* people. If they are anything like the ones who come here to Bath to take the waters I'll be horrendously bored all the time.'

'You'll meet lots of eligible young men, and you know that's what the Season's about, finding a husband.'

'Humph! I don't want to be paraded at Almack's so that all the men on the catch for a wife can inspect me, as if I were a horse. I'm not interested in getting married. What I'd really like is a small cottage in the country and to be able to breed dogs.'

'Not more misbegotten curs like the one you already have, please. You should have little ones old ladies like for company, like pugs or spaniels.'

'Rusty is not misbegotten! Just because you don't know what breed he is there's no need to sneer at him.'

'Breed? He could lay claim to at least six, I think, and even you provide him with a different ancestry every time you're asked.'

She giggled. 'Well, it depends who asks. I can imagine a Scottish terrier for a Scotsman, or a Welsh corgi, or a poodle for a Frenchman. Isn't that the sort of tact Aunt Emily is always talking about? I wish I could meet a Russian, I love those hunting dogs

3

they have. Those are the sort I'd like to breed.'

'Whatever breed you fancy you can't do that.'

'Why not? Someone has to.'

'Not you, brat. In the first place, you couldn't live alone. In the second, the idea of an unmarried female having anything to do with breeding, dogs or anything else, is quite unacceptable to genteel people. And in the third, they're all afraid we'll fall in love and want to get married. They want to see you safely hitched to someone more eligible.'

Abby hooted with laughter. 'Marry you? When we've been like brother and sister, and know one another's most disreputable secrets? It would never work. In any event, what has it to do with my being able to breed dogs? Unless,' she added speculatively, 'they think we might do it together.'

He grinned at her. 'It's never going to. I don't want a mad-brained firebrand for a wife, thank you, and there's nothing I'd like worse than being surrounded by dogs. Horses, perhaps, but you can't tell an Arab from a carthorse.'

'I can ride either, but how gallant of you, Hartley dear, when I haven't even proposed to you.' She paused, thinking. 'I suppose they are afraid we might run away to Gretna Green, like my parents did.'

'They need not be concerned. I wouldn't do anything in such deplorable taste.'

She flared up. 'So that's what you think of my parents, is it? Thank you, Hartley, I'm glad I know your opinion of them. Mama's parents were utterly unreasonable, refusing her permission to marry a perfectly respectable man just because they wanted her to marry a horrid neighbour and unite the two estates. I think they were sensible to elope, since they loved each other so much. I only wish I'd known them, but they died before I could even remember them at all.'

'Oh Lord, I didn't mean to upset you. I'm sorry, Abby. Look, oughtn't you to be going home instead of bandying words with me? I saw that trustee of yours arriving when I left the house. No doubt he'll want to see you.'

'Mr Wood? Why didn't you say so instead of keeping me here? Really, Hartley, you have no sense of priorities. Like you have no taste in choosing a waistcoat, or notion of how to tie a cravat,' she flung over her shoulder as she picked up her skirts and began to run towards Henrietta Street.

* * *

Mr Wood sipped the Madeira his hostess had poured for him. They were sitting in the small room off the entrance hall, used as a library and office, in which she sat most of the time in preference to the more formal drawing room on the next floor.

'You say she can be ready by the end of the week, Emily?'

'It's rather sudden, and I haven't bought her enough gowns yet. I assumed I'd have a few more weeks,' Lady Jordan said, twisting the cambric handkerchief in her agitated fingers.

'Hester Padmore proposes to travel to London tomorrow, and I'd rather Abby were with her as soon as possible, before she begins to take Caroline about. I don't want Abby to feel at a disadvantage, not knowing people.'

'Certainly not, I wouldn't wish that on her, Laurence. She needs to feel comfortable with everyone. But you're paying Lady Padmore an outrageous sum; she won't dare to cheat you, however poor she thinks herself. And Lord Padmore did leave her in straightened circumstances. He gambled away such a lot, as you know.'

'He was a fool. Men who can't afford to lose ought not to hazard their patrimony.'

'Oh. No. Of course not,' she replied.

'And you need not be concerned about clothes; Abby can order what she likes, and

Hester Padmore knows she's to be turned out in the best style. She'll have me to answer to if she tries to skimp or make her own girl look better turned out.'

'What's Caroline like? Is she a beauty? Hester was in her day, but I haven't been to London for over a decade, and haven't seen her for over twenty years, since she married Lord Padmore. Even then I didn't know her well, she was a few years older than I.'

'She's pretty in a way, a rather insipid blonde. Not a striking redhead like Abby.'

'Auburn, or Titian, please, not red, Laurence. Brighter than poor Louisa's hair, if her portrait is to be believed, but not red.'

'If you say. How are matters with young Hartley?'

'They're still together far more than I like. He goes riding and walking with her, and has stood up with her at every Assembly and private ball we've been to.'

'Can't you head him off? It wouldn't do; his family are tradesmen, nobodies. Abby is too good for marriage with a tradesman. She's entitled to mix with the best.'

'I can't make too much fuss in case it gives them ideas. It's a pity he lives next door, but I hope when she's in London she'll have other things to think about.'

'And more eligible men making up to her. I

want her to have the best; it's her right. Someone who will accept her unreservedly,' he added, almost to himself.

Lady Jordan sighed. 'Someone she can love, I hope. Like I did. I'm afraid Hester married for position, but from what I hear it's brought her neither comfort nor satisfaction.'

He nodded, but he was listening to the sound of voices in the hall outside the library, and smiling.

'Here she is now, I think.'

As he spoke the door opened and Abby came into the room impetuously, almost ran across to him and, as he stood up to greet her, flung herself into his arms.

'Mr Wood, I didn't know you were coming today. I'd have been at home to greet you. How are you? What are you doing here in Bath? Is everything all right? Has Lady Padmore decided she doesn't want to be bothered with me after all?'

'Abby!' Lady Jordan said reprovingly, but with a laugh in her voice.

He laughed and held her away from him.

'You get prettier by the day, more and more like your poor mother.'

'Do I?' Her voice was wistful. 'I don't believe I'm a bit like that miniature portrait of her you gave me for my last birthday. Oh, Aunt Emily, I'm sorry, but I'm so pleased to see Mr Wood, and so hoping he's come to say I needn't be dragged to London after all.'

'I'm sorry, Abby, but I want you to be in London on Friday. I'm putting up at the Pelican, and we'll set out early on Thursday. I'm planning to stay at either Marlborough or Hungerford, as I don't want you to be too fagged when you get to London.'

He watched her smile fade, but hardened his heart. It was her due, to make a respectable marriage, and she was unlikely to meet suitable men here in Bath. He would be failing in his duty to her dead mother if he did not provide her with the best opportunities.

'Very well,' she said, suppressing a sigh. 'But I won't marry anyone I don't like.'

'No one would expect that, child,' Lady Jordan said. 'Whatever gave you the idea you might be so persuaded?'

'But girls have to do as they're told, don't they?'

Mr Wood suppressed a grin.

'Your mother didn't, and you're very like her, Abby. I cannot imagine you agreeing to marry anyone unless you loved him.'

She beamed at him. 'Well, I'm sure I won't find anyone like that in London, so why do I have to go?'

He groaned. 'Abigail, just try, will you?'

She dimpled. 'I know you are getting cross

with me when you call me Abigail. May I take Rusty to London?'

'Your dog? Won't he be a nuisance? He's no lapdog.'

'I won't even consider anyone who doesn't like him. That shall be my test. You are insisting my groom comes with me, as well as Ellie, so when I can't look after him George can.'

'Poor George! The last time I encountered the animal he had just had a fight with another dog and had come off rather the worse for wear.'

'That was a huge mastiff! It was twice his size. Rusty did very well, and tore off part of his ear!'

He laughed. 'All right, bring the brute.'

'Oh, thank you! You are the very best trustee a girl ever had!' she exclaimed, catching his hand in hers and kissing it.

His laughing protests were cut short as the door opened and a large dog, whose fur was almost the same colour as Abby's hair, erupted into the room, plumed tail wagging wildly. Mr Wood swiftly rescued his glass of Madeira from the low table before the dog's tail could sweep it to the floor.

'Abby!' Lady Jordan exclaimed. 'I thought he was tied up in the stables while you were out.'

'He was, but George saw me come back and must have let him go. Down, Rusty!'

Rather to Mr Wood's surprise the dog instantly lay down, panting, his tongue lolling, and looking adoringly at his mistress.

'Let us hope Lady Padmore likes dogs, however well behaved.'

'She must, or I shall refuse to stay with her.'

'Abby,' Lady Jordan protested, but weakly.

Mr Wood shook his head but did not chastise her.

'You can be packed in time? I'll hire a carriage big enough for all your luggage.'

'I don't have much. All my gowns are childish, and Aunt Emily says I need to buy more modish ones in London.'

'You can buy what you like there, you'll have an ample allowance. We should be able to reach Hill Street by early evening on Friday.'

* * *

Two days later Abby's maid Ellie was packing the last of her gowns, carefully folding them with tissue, when Lady Jordan came into the bedroom.

'Abby, come along to my boudoir, dear. I have something for you.'

When they were in the prettily furnished and decorated room, with its pale-pink flowered wallpaper and deeper pink curtains, she gestured to Abby to draw a stool up beside her own dressing stool.

'These were your mother's,' she said, taking some flat, velvet-covered boxes from one of the drawers and handing them to Abby. 'Mr Wood wants you to have them now. There are more, but these are suitable for a debutante. Well, won't you look at them?'

Abby swallowed the incipient tears and began to open the boxes. In the first was a single row of pearls, and matching bracelet and ear-drops. She gasped.

'These are lovely, and so big! Much bigger than Cordelia Blackstone's, and she's very proud of them. She wears them all the time — I expect she wears them in bed too.'

She opened another box, revealing an intricately linked gold chain from which depended a single large diamond in a gold setting. Here, too, were matching ear-drops, and simple gold bracelets. In the third box was a necklace of opals, and in a fourth one of coral and another of some green stones.

'What are these?' Abby asked. 'They are pretty, but this one is not emeralds, nor jade, I think.'

'It's malachite. These two are less valuable,

but they will suit you. The rubies and sapphires are in the bank, and will be yours in a few years, when you are married, or old enough to wear them.'

She turned to another drawer in the dressing table and abstracted another box.

'This is from me, amethysts. They belonged to my mother, but they are exactly the colour of your eyes, so I want you to have them.'

Abby flung her arms round Lady Jordan and hugged her convulsively.

'Oh, you are so good to me! But why do I have to go to London?'

'It's your birthright, my dear. Your mother was a lady, and Mr Wood wishes you to have every advantage you would have had if she had lived.'

Abby sighed. 'I know so little about my parents, except that they ran away to Gretna Green, and her family disowned her. I don't even know if my grandparents are still alive, or if I have any other relatives. My father had no close relatives, I know. But you have been like a mother to me, and I couldn't have loved my own mother more!'

Lady Jordan wiped away a tear from her own eyes.

'I had no children, but you've been my daughter since you were two years old, when Mr Wood brought you to us. Lord Jordan loved you too. It's a great shame he did not live to see what a beautiful girl you've become.'

Abby chuckled. 'Me, beautiful? With this mop of red hair, and freckles when I've been out in the sun?'

'Cucumber, my dear. But — '

'Prevention is better than cure,' Abby said, and they laughed.

Abby grew thoughtful again.

'Was it really just because my grandparents wanted Mama to marry a neighbour's son, or did they disapprove of my father? What was wrong with him? It couldn't have been because he was poor. He must have left a large enough fortune to provide for me, for my allowance is generous, and Mr Wood told me it was to be increased while I am in London.'

'Truly, Abby, I have no notion whether they disapproved of him, or were just determined your mama would marry where they chose. I never knew them. But you must forget the past, it's the future you have to consider. Now run along to bed, it's late and you have to be up early tomorrow.'

★　★　★

Abby was rather silent during the first hour or so of the journey to London, inhibited perhaps by Ellie's presence on the forward seat. Rusty, at Abby's insistence, sprawled untidily on the floor between them while George rode on the box with the coachman. She had taken a rather tearful farewell from Lady Jordan, who had promised to visit her in London in a few weeks' time.

She had never been further from Bath than Bristol, and rarely been apart from Lady Jordan. It was the first time she had been away from home alone, and she was wondering how she would manage, whether she would like Caroline, and whether Caroline would like her.

She was apprehensive about being in London, as well as wondering how she would get on with Lady Padmore and her daughter. It was a new experience to be so uncertain. Normally, Abby got on well with everyone and had no qualms about meeting new people, but fashionable London people were new to her, and she had not liked some of the dandies and fops who occasionally graced Bath with their presence, and uttered false compliments.

She knew her trustees were paying the lady to introduce her to Society along with Caroline, who was a month or so younger than Abby, and suspected her hostess might regard her as a necessary but inconvenient guest. She had gathered that Lady Padmore, despite being the cousin of a wealthy man, was not very flush in the pocket. The late Lord Padmore had, like Lord Jordan, been an old friend of Mr Wood's. She thought they had all been at school together, but whenever she asked about his family he always turned the conversation to something else, though occasionally she had surprised a wistful look in his eyes. Perhaps there was something disreputable in his family, though if that were so she would like it rather than disapprove.

Her thoughts swung to Caroline, with whom she was to be presented. What sort of girl was she? Would they become friends? Or, and the thought made her chuckle, would they become rivals, either for the attentions of the same man, or being the first to attract an offer.

She did not want to marry, but despite her protests to Hartley and Mr Wood, accepted it was the only course for a girl to take. She began to speculate on what sort of offers she might obtain. She was an orphan, and had, she understood from Mr Wood, a reasonable expectation, if not a huge fortune. He had refused to be more precise, saying he would discuss that with any prospective suitor. He wanted her husband to love her without any regard to her portion.

After the first few miles Abby's natural resilience asserted itself, and she began to take notice of the countryside and the villages they passed through, and to demand to know all about the people she could expect to meet in London.

'Caroline's father is dead, isn't he, so her brother is Lord Padmore? How old is he?'

'Dudley is a couple of years older than Caroline, twenty and a few months. He does not reach his majority until later this year. He is presently with the army, waiting to go to India. His cousin, Lord Keighley, is his guardian and trustee.'

'Does he live in London too? Will I meet him? Is he old?'

'He's eight and twenty, and has a house in Grosvenor Square.'

'That's young to be a guardian.'

'His father was Dudley Padmore's guardian until his death three years ago. Julian Keighley resigned his commission in the guards and came home then. He has no heir apart from a distant cousin, but he shows no inclination to set up his nursery yet.'

'Why should he if he doesn't wish to? Why does it matter who inherits a title and money? When one is dead, one ceases to care, I imagine.'

'True, but most people want to make sure

their money and land go to someone close to them. And if one has children, one tries to provide for them.'

By the time they reached the posting inn at Hungerford where they were to spend the night she was beginning to look forward to being in London, and on the following day as they entered the outskirts of the capital late in the afternoon she became more excited. It was so different from Bath, where there were relatively few coaches in the town, because of the steep hills, and so much noisier with the press of wheeled traffic, the coaches and curricles and laden wagons and carts which were far more numerous than she had seen even in Bristol.

Abby was silent, gazing in awe at the houses they passed as they entered the streets of Mayfair. There were many new buildings in Bath, and she was familiar with the modern architectural designs, but she had not really appreciated just how large London was. When they passed through Grosvenor Square she looked round in amazement at the large expanse.

'There is nothing like this in Bath, the squares there are tiny. And these houses are like palaces,' she said. 'Lord Keighley has one of them, you say?'

'That one on that corner,' Mr Wood said,

gesturing. 'It's one of the largest. You won't find the house in Hill Street nearly so large, but that is hired, it does not belong to Lady Padmore. They sold their London house some years ago.'

'When her husband lost money gambling,' Abby said, nodding. 'I do think hazarding money on the turn of a card or the throw of dice is a stupid pastime.'

'Do you, my dear?'

'Well, I suppose it can be exciting, but whole estates are lost, and men are ruined.' She paused. 'But if one man loses another must win. I suppose that's what they all hope for.'

'Women gamble too,' he said gently. 'The late Duchess of Devonshire, the beautiful Georgiana, lost thousands at the tables.'

'It's perhaps fortunate I don't have thousands to lose, and I detest card games, they are so tedious,' she said. 'Are we almost there? I think you said Hill Street was quite close to Grosvenor Square.'

2

Julian Keighley, Earl of Wantock, sanded his letter just as Denton, his butler, entered the library.

'My lord, Lady Jane and Lady Padmore have called.'

'At this hour? What the devil do they want?' The earl glanced at the ormulo clock on the mantelpiece and saw that it was not quite ten o'clock.

'And Lady Jane has brought her youngest son with her.'

The earl groaned. 'Not that obnoxious little devil we caught tying a rope across the top of the back stairs!'

'I'm afraid it is the Honourable Peter, my lord.'

'Show them into the drawing room.'

'Yes, my lord. I have done so. But the fire there has not been lit.'

'Good man! What would I do without you, Denton? Now perhaps they won't stay long. I'll go straight up.'

Denton coughed, and glanced meaningly at the earl's vividly patterned dressing gown which he wore over breeches and a snowy white shirt.

The earl laughed. 'You think they'll be offended? Even better.'

He ran up the stairs to the first floor, grinning. He was engaged to ride out with some friends at eleven, if, that was, they managed to rouse themselves out of bed by that time. Last night had been a late one, the cards had been disobliging, and the wine had flowed freely.

What did his sister and their cousin want now? he wondered, throwing open the door of the drawing room and discovering Lady Jane on her knees trying to encourage the paper and sticks laid in the fireplace to ignite. She turned to face him, her face unbecomingly flushed, a frown in her blue eyes. She was not ageing well, he thought. She had been a beauty at eighteen, but now, almost forty, she had gained weight, and the discontented expression she usually wore had left deep grooves on her face.

As she began to struggle to her feet he moved to help her, but his attention switched to his young nephew, who was engaged in collecting together on one sopha all the small ornaments, most of them valuable Meissen or Bow ware, which Julian's mother delighted in displaying on numerous small tables. Praying none of them had been chipped, he swooped down on Peter and lifted the boy away from the danger area. Peter promptly gave vent to a furious wail and hammered his small fists against his uncle's face. The earl was compelled to set him down on his feet, while he clasped the flailing arms to the boy's sides.

'If you bring this hellion into the house you might ensure he does no damage, Jane! Mama will be distressed if he has damaged any of her precious mementoes.'

He handed the squirming child to Lady Jane, who had gained her feet and was approaching hurriedly.

'There wouldn't have been the temptation if we'd been shown into the back parlour, where there is no doubt a fire I don't have to light, so that I can keep an eye on the poor sweet.'

The earl turned to greet the other lady, who was seated on another sopha, clutching her pelisse to her and shivering. A few years older than his sister, she had worn better, but he decided this was due to severe corseting and the clever and discreet application of cosmetics.

'Lady Padmore, how good of you to call. So early too. You are fortunate, Jane, to find me out of bed.'

'But not properly attired for receiving visitors,' she said, eying the dressing gown with disapproval.

'I would have taken the time to tie my cravat before coming in, had I not thought you would not care to wait an hour or so in a cold room.'

'Fop!'

Before she had time to enlarge on this frequent accusation her son, who had been eyeing the earl resentfully, spoke.

'Why are you wearing a dress, Uncle Julian?'

He suppressed a grin. 'This is not a dress, my lad. Doesn't your papa have dressing gowns?'

'Oh, that is beside the point! Julian, I came to ask you to reconsider your disobliging refusal to open up the ballroom for young Caroline's dance. She's family, and has a right to use it.'

'She may be family, Jane, but what about this child you are sponsoring, Cousin Hester? She's not family, is she?'

'Of course not, but that's irrelevant. It need not disturb you unduly, Cousin Julian,' Lady Padmore said. 'Mr Wood will pay for the hire of extra servants to prepare the room, and we will bring in all the refreshments.'

'Mr Wood being this chit's banker, I take it? So her presence is in fact essential to your arrangements? Rather relevant, I would have thought.'

'You are being perverse, Julian!' Lady Jane said. 'We are merely asking for the use of the ballroom.'

'And rooms for cards, sitting out, cloak-rooms, refreshments perhaps?'

'What does that matter? You need do nothing.'

'Except take myself to a hotel for a week beforehand! No, Cousin Hester. I was only eight at the time, but I well recall the upheaval on the occasion of Jane's ball. The whole house was in turmoil for weeks beforehand, and afterwards. I suppose the house in Hill Street is not large enough. But if Mr Wood is being so generous why can you not hire a public room?'

'It looks so shabby! And the more people we are able to invite the more likely we will be able to get Caroline and this other girl off creditably.'

'Mr Wood's ward, I take it. When does she arrive, this mysterious girl, whose background and birth you know nothing about? I confess I was surprised to hear you were becoming an employee of a City stock jobber, Hester.'

She flushed. 'I am merely doing him a favour, Julian. I don't think he's really a jobber; he just has interests in the City. I get no benefit.'

'Except the hire of a house in the best part

of town, and no doubt some other perks such as servants and carriages.'

'I wouldn't have needed to do it if you hadn't refused to let us stay here. You know what straits Henry left us in. We have barely enough to live on after he gambled most of it away. And he knew Mr Wood, who is perfectly respectable!'

'I dare say. But you know nothing about the girl, whether she is presentable, who her family are.'

'She's been brought up in Bath by Emily Jordan, and though I haven't seen Emily for many years, she is respectable enough. The girl is not likely to disgrace us.'

'If you say so. When does she arrive?'

'This afternoon. Oh well, Jane, if Julian is going to be disobliging, I suppose I had better go and consider other options.'

She rose to leave, and the earl bowed to her as he rang for Denton.

'You are monstrously high in the instep, Julian,' Lady Jane said, as she swept past him, 'and I shall take care not to ask for any favours if you refuse them in such a manner!'

'Good. I'll remember that, my dear sister, even if you don't. Ah, Denton, show the ladies out if you please.'

He watched them leave, hardening his heart, then went upstairs to finish dressing.

Until he had succeeded to the earldom three years before, Jane had made maximum use of her ten years' superiority in age to criticize everything he did. Then she had paid lip service to him as head of the family, while phrasing her criticisms as helpful suggestions as to how he ought to conduct his life and, in particular, how he owed it to the family to improve its fortunes by marrying an heiress. If she were unable to present him to suitable wealthy candidates for his hand she pointed them out to him, with instructions on how best he might obtain introductions.

So far he had met no girl to keep his interest for more than a few days. Since his fortune, despite Jane's opinion, was perfectly adequate, and he had no particular urge to marry, and none whatsoever to set up his nursery if all children were like Jane's, he was quite content to ignore her suggestions and, after brief polite conversations, and perhaps one or two invitations to dance, treat the selected damsels with cool indifference. All of them bored him. They either flirted unbecomingly or had little to say for themselves, simpered or giggled at his remarks, and utterly failed to understand his references to political or literary matters. Since politics absorbed much of his attention, and he read widely amongst the classics as well as contemporary novels and poetry, he had occasionally wondered what on earth they would have conversed about, had he ever married one of them.

Hester, who was only a distant cousin, had been inclined to censure him on every occasion they met. She disapproved of his clothes, his friends, his predilection, as she called it, for all forms of sport, and his political opinions. When his father had died tragically young she had changed her attitude, and lost no opportunity of thrusting her daughter, at that time a timid damsel of fifteen, under his notice. He was well aware she hoped to marry him to the chit. He liked Caroline and was sorry for her, but not enough to gratify her mother by lending his house for her ball. As for marriage, she tempted him not at all. She was too quiet, too insipid, too likely to turn out like her mother. At the thought he shuddered.

He had met Mr Wood, and knew he was a wealthy man. If he were sponsoring some unknown girl into Society, he would provide lavishly for her. As a bachelor he could not do it himself, even though he lived in a large house in St James's Square, so it was reasonable he would employ some lady of quality to perform the task.

Going down to the stables to fetch his

mount, he thrust all thoughts of Jane and Hester from his mind. He and two friends were riding out to Epsom to try out the paces of a new horse one of them had just acquired, and later would dine at a favoured hostelry on the way home. That was the sort of day he preferred, one which Jane and Hester heartily condemned.

★ ★ ★

When the chaise stopped outside Lady Padmore's house Abby took a deep breath and looked at Mr Wood.

'You won't desert me too soon, will you?' she asked.

'How can you ask? My dear, I am sure you will like Caroline, and her mother will do all she can to make you feel at home. But if there are any problems, you can send George with a message to me in the City, and I will come straight to you.'

'I am not afraid, but I don't know how to go on it Society, and perhaps I'll let you all down.'

'Just be your delightful self,' Mr Wood replied.

Abby chuckled. 'You cannot know me very well, sir! But it was a pretty compliment. I have an unfortunate habit of saying what I think without considering whether it will offend. Hartley was always telling me to pause before I spoke.'

'Hartley has been a good friend, has he not?'

'He's almost the only young person in Bath that I can talk to, who shares my own tastes in poetry, and laughs at the same things.'

'I am sure you will find more such friends in London.'

'Well, I hope so, but the sooner Hartley comes to Town the better.'

'Comes to Town? You mean he is following you?'

Abby chuckled again. 'No, of course not. He always intended to come this year, now he has come of age and into his inheritance. It was decided before you told me I was to come, but it will be pleasant to have someone from home I can talk to.'

'Of course, but you must not spend too much time with him. You need to meet other people, make new friends.'

'And find a husband,' Abby said, and sighed. 'If I don't, may I go back to Bath, sir?'

He took her hands in his. 'Abby, my dear, I have no desire to persuade you into marriage unless you meet a man you can love without reservation. Like your mother did. But how could you meet enough young men in Bath to have a proper choice? You deserve this chance. But come, they have opened the door and are waiting for us.'

He rarely spoke of her mother, and would never tell her anything about her grandparents, saying she would be better off forgetting them. She supposed the scandal of their elopement was a disgrace which would reflect on her. One day, she promised herself, she would persuade him to tell her more, but now was not the time.

The next few minutes were somewhat confused. As the steps were let down Rusty, tired of the confinement, leaped out first and before George had descended from the box had streaked up the road in pursuit of a cat.

'Oh, he'll be hurt!' Abby exclaimed, and leaped down after him. She put two fingers to her mouth and let out a piercing whistle. Rusty hesitated, then turned and slunk back to her. Abby patted him and slipped the rope collar over his head and handed the end of the rope to George. Then she turned to one of the footmen, standing beside the chaise.

'Please can you show my groom where the stables are, so that he can take Rusty there? I don't imagine he'd be welcome in a drawing room.'

Mr Wood had descended from the chaise, and took her arm to guide her up the steps into the house where she was met by a tall, thin butler. Inclining his head he indicated they were to follow him and led the way up the stairs and into a drawing room, where Abby found three ladies waiting for her. For a moment they stared at her, making no move to come forward. Abby flung up her head and stared back, determined not to be intimidated. Then the eldest of the ladies rose to her feet and approached.

'My dear Miss Barton, welcome to London. I trust you had a comfortable journey? This is Lady Jane Ilroy, a distant cousin, and my daughter Caroline.'

Abby dipped into a curtsy to the older ladies, and smiled at Caroline. She was pretty, Abby saw, with fluffy blonde curls framing a pale, heart-shaped face, and big blue eyes. She looked rather apprehensive, and Abby was tempted to ask what she was frightened of. Heeding the advice of Hartley to pause, she bit back the words and turned her attention back to her hostess.

'It's very good of you to invite me here, Lady Padmore,' she said. 'Do I call you my chaperon, or duenna?'

Lady Padmore blinked. 'Well, I suppose I am your chaperon, but so I am to Caroline. A duenna is more like a paid governess, I think, and I am not being paid like that, you know.

Mr Wood's money is for financing your come-out.'

'I thought you were being paid — Oh dear, I am sorry.'

Mr Wood interposed quickly.

'It would be best for you to refer to Lady Padmore as your hostess, Abby.'

'Yes, of course.'

Lady Padmore was frowning, and Abby sighed inwardly. She had scarcely entered the house and she had managed to offend the woman. How was she to endure three months of watching what she said every moment of the day?

'Caroline will show you to your room, Abigail. And when you have tidied yourself we will have tea. I have not accepted any invitations for tonight, as I supposed you would like an early night after your journey. You must be tired.'

Caroline, with an anxious look at her mother, led the way from the room and up another flight of stairs.

'I do hope we'll be friends,' she said breathlessly, as she opened the door into a small, but prettily decorated bedroom. 'It will be fun to go to dances together. I hate meeting new people, I never know what to say to them.'

'You're talking to me,' Abby said. 'I'm sure

you will manage. I do like this room, and I'm sure we will be friends. I am not looking forward to all this fuss, but we can sympathize with each other.'

'But we have to do it,' Caroline sighed, wandering across to look out of the window towards the opposite houses, 'for how else can we meet a man to marry? Look, I put some flowers here for you, on the dressing table.'

'Thank you, they are pretty.'

'I bought them while we were out this morning. Mama was leaving cards at all our acquaintances, to let them know where we are living. Do you have cards to leave?'

'I don't know anyone in London,' Abby said, laughing.

She was busy removing her travelling cloak, and washing her hands in the water someone had poured into the washbasin.

'Neither do I, but Mama says we will soon have lots of acquaintances once the Season proper starts.'

'Is Lady Jane a friend of your mother's?' Abby asked. 'Did she say she was a cousin? I wasn't listening, I'm afraid.'

'I think my grandmother and Cousin Jane's mother were sisters, but I am not entirely sure. Oh, look. Abigail, someone has already unpacked your hairbrushes. Would you like me to brush your hair? It's a lovely colour. I wish I were a brunette instead of this insipid yellow.'

'It's not insipid, and you don't get teased and called names because of it! And please call me Abby. I always feel people are annoyed with me when they use my full name. So Lady Jane is a sort of cousin?'

Caroline frowned in concentration as she picked up the hairbrush and began to smooth Abby's rebellious curls.

'My great-grandfather was married three times, so I'm not certain. My grandmother and her mother might have been half-sisters. I find all this family business so confusing, and so many people one meets are related in some way to one another!'

Abby grinned at her. 'There were some old ladies in Bath who seemed to spend all their time tracing family connections. They didn't get far with me, I don't even know who my grandparents were.'

Caroline stopped brushing and stared at Abby's reflection in the dressing-table mirror.

'You don't know your grandparents?' she asked. 'But how, why not?'

'My parents eloped to Gretna Green, and my mother's family cast her off. My father was an orphan. They both died before I was old enough to ask questions, and no one else will tell me. I'm sure Aunt Emily doesn't know, or I could have persuaded her. Mr Wood knows — he's my trustee — but he refuses, says I am better off not knowing who they are, and I suppose I am since they were so cruel to my mama.'

Caroline's eyes were wide with shock.

'How romantic! To elope, I mean. But how horrid not to know your family! Why, you might meet them here in London and not know.'

'I'd rather not know. Ought we to go back downstairs? Your mama will be wondering what we are doing.'

* * *

Lord Wantock was thoughtful as he rode towards home. The projected ride to Epsom had been postponed halfway there when his friend's horse had picked up a stone and become lame. Seeing a travelling chaise drawn up in front of Lady Padmore's hired house he had paused, suspecting it was her unknown guest arriving. Then, as a blur of red fur shot past him he was fully occupied for a couple of minutes controlling his mount, who objected strongly to dogs.

A piercing whistle made him glance at the chaise, and he blinked. Surely it could not be that girl standing beside it who had made such a noise? It had taken him years, as a boy, to acquire such a whistle, and he was not at all sure he could produce it to order.

The dog, he was amused to see, was slinking back, tail between its legs, and abasing itself before the girl. As she bent to pat it the hood of her cloak fell back, and he wondered if he was imagining things. Her hair was almost the same colour as the dog's coat. Then she turned, and while a man, presumably a groom, led the dog away, she went into the house. He recognized Mr Wood. As the door was closed on them he rode home in a thoughtful mood. So that was Hester's guest, the girl she was to introduce to the *ton*. Striking in looks, from the little he had seen of her, and unconventional. He knew of no other girl who could have produced that whistle. He would call on Cousin Hester in the morning.

Before he could do that, however, he encountered the girl and the dog again. He frequently rode in the Park early in the morning, and he was trotting through the gate when he saw them a short distance away.

He frowned, for she appeared to be on her own. The dog, he was thankful to see, was securely attached to a rope, and though the animal was clearly eager to be freed and racing after squirrels, it obeyed the girl and walked decorously at her side.

Now he could see her properly, for she wore only a dark-green spencer over a simple morning gown of pale jonquil. Her figure was shapely, and her face arrestingly lovely. From this distance he could not see the colour of her eyes, but he suspected they would be green. He had always favoured that colouring, and his last mistress had known it and heightened the sandy colour of her hair with henna. But she was past history. When he had made it clear he had no intention of marrying her she had swiftly found herself a rich merchant and married him.

He drew rein behind some trees and watched, intrigued, when the girl stopped. She was holding some sort of cane, and after a moment he realized she was trying to teach the dog to jump over it. She was patient, showing the dog what was expected by putting down the cane on the grass and jumping over it herself, encouraging the animal to jump with her. It was obviously an intelligent creature, for it soon caught on, and she gradually raised the cane until it was waist high.

She hugged the dog and gave it something from her pocket, then walked backwards for a couple of yards while the dog walked towards her on its hind legs.

Then the earl saw he was not the only interested observer. A young man he knew slightly, riding a showy black, was watching.

'Training him for the circus, are you?' the man called, and urged his horse forward until he was just a couple of yards from the girl. 'Are you a trapeze artiste? I can imagine you in spangled tights. Or perhaps you do acrobatic stunts on galloping ponies? How about a private exhibition? I'll pay you well, my dear.'

The girl glanced at him, then said something the earl could not hear. She let go the rope lead and instantly her dog became a growling, menacing ball of fury, and hurled himself at the man, whose horse reared in fright and deposited him on the ground before galloping off.

A short command, and the dog returned to her side. With a contemptuous look at the fallen man she turned on her heel and walked slowly away. Her eyes, he now saw, were not green, but an enchanting shade of violet.

Julian watched in amusement as the fellow rose to his feet and looked round for his horse, which had come to a halt a long way in the distance. He began to hobble towards it, and the earl turned away and continued his ride. He had a great deal to think about.

On the following morning he considered whether to pay a visit to Lady Padmore. He had suffered a restless night, as visions of red-haired beauties insisted on intruding into his dreams. At breakfast he finally decided he wished to get to know this unconventional girl better. He arrived in Hill Street just as the ladies returned from a shopping expedition, and found the narrow hall cluttered with many parcels. Hester was wasting no time spending Mr Wood's money, he thought.

The butler showed him into the drawing room, where the ladies were about to have a reviving cup of tea.

Lady Padmore looked across at him, puzzled.

'Julian? To what do we owe this pleasure?'

He smiled at her, but his main attention was for the girl seated beside her. Yes, she was as lovely as he had supposed, and her eyes, candidly observing him, were violet.

'Will you not introduce me to your guest?' he asked softly.

He accepted a cup of tea, a beverage he normally despised, and ate a dainty confection which he recognized as one of Gunter's standard cakes. The girl, he now knew, was called Abigail, and she was full of questions about what she ought to see while in London.

'For I expect it will be my only visit,' she

explained, 'and I have to make the most of it before I return to Bath.'

Suddenly he made up his mind.

'Oh, I'm sure you will make many more visits. But Hester, what I came to say was that I was rather curt the other day. My only excuse is that I was preoccupied with some problems to do with the estate. I have reconsidered: you may use my ballroom for Caroline's ball.'

3

Caroline could hardly wait to leave the drawing room once Julian had left. She dragged Abby upstairs and into her bedroom. She danced around the room while Abby sat on the bed and watched her in amusement.

'Why are you so excited?'

'Oh, Abby! I do love Cousin Julian! How utterly marvellous of him! We'll be able to ask two hundred people, perhaps more. After what he said the other day too. I wonder what has changed his mind?'

'What did he say the other day?'

'It was the day you arrived. Mama had been to see him that morning to ask him to lend us his ballroom for our dance, and he said nothing would persuade him to. She was furious with him, called him odiously top lofty, and vowed she would not be forced to hire a public room. But I don't know what else she could have done. No one else we know would lend theirs, and anyway, Julian's is much the largest.'

Abby frowned. 'Why should he lend his ballroom? And why does it matter where the dance is held?'

'Of course it matters. It would be horrid and penny-pinching if we had to have some beastly public ballroom. Why, most of the best people would not bother to come.'

Abby shrugged. 'Just because it was not held in some private house?'

'You don't understand. It's not just the ballroom, we will be able to have card rooms for the older people, and tables set up for supper in the dining room and the parlours and the conservatory. It will be so much more comfortable, and Cousin Julian's house is furnished in the most delightful style. After his papa died he threw out all the old, really ugly furniture, and had the entire house decorated, and bought modern furniture.'

'Then I'm not surprised he doesn't want hundreds of people in his house! I know what a great deal of work it takes to have just a small party, like the ones Aunt Emily has for no more than a dozen or so guests.'

'He didn't, at first, but he's clearly decided to be generous to us. He absolutely refused to let us live there for my come out, but Mama thought he would let us have my dance there. Perhaps his mama has persuaded him. Oh, this is becoming the most exciting season, and I thought it was going to be so utterly grim, if we could only afford to rent a house in Bloomsbury, with all the merchants and clerks and people who work in the City.'

'I don't understand. What's wrong with Bloomsbury, and merchants?'

Caroline laughed. 'It's not at all fashionable. If we were living there, no one of any importance would invite us anywhere, and they would not pay morning calls, or acknowledge us. We'd never have a chance of meeting eligible young men. But the money your trustees provided has enabled us to hire this house, in a much better part of town. Of course, it's mainly for your benefit, so that you get to know the right people and make a good marriage, but I shall benefit too, you see. That's why Mama agreed to do it.'

Abby did see, and she wondered just how much more expensive it was to hire a house in Hill Street instead of this unacceptable Bloomsbury. Mr Wood seemed to be spending a great deal to give her a come out which would ensure she found a husband. She sighed. Perhaps it was her duty to him and all his care for her to do as they all so clearly wished and accept her fate. She was, however, determined to have some say in the choice of whoever became that husband. He would have to be compliant, someone who would not interfere with her pursuits, nor expect her to spend all her time entertaining boring people. Most of all he must accept her

as she was, not try to make her conform, as
her friend Hannah Wilkes's husband had
done the moment they were married. Jonah
Wilkes, it seemed to Abby, never stopped
telling Hannah how to behave, what to say,
with whom she might be friends — even what
she must wear.

★ ★ ★

Lady Padmore normally had breakfast in
bed, and did not emerge from her bedroom
until noon. A few days later, though, she sent
a message to the breakfast room bidding
Abby attend her at once.

Wondering at the summons, Abby went
upstairs, knocked at her hostess's bedroom
door, and was bidden, in a faint voice, to
enter.

She found Lady Padmore, swathed in
clouds of chiffon and lace, sitting upright in
her bed and surrounded by what looked like
calling cards and invitations. Her maid, a
plump girl with a north-country accent, was
displaying various gowns, apparently for her
mistress's approval.

'No, Joan, not the puce satin. Leave it now,
I'll ring when I need you.'

Joan left the room, and Lady Padmore
pointed to a chair set beside the bed.

'Please sit down, Abigail. I'm afraid that animal you have inflicted on us, without my permission, has been terrorizing the horses. This morning he caused a good deal of commotion by chasing the stable cat. You must send him back to Bath. I can't understand why a sensible woman like Emily Jordan permits you to have such a brute.'

'Rusty is not a brute!' Abby said, leaping up from the chair she had just sat down in. 'He does not frighten horses unless they are silly animals who take exception to everything! And if he managed to chase the cat, which is something every dog does if it has any spirit, one of the grooms must have let him out of the loose box he sleeps in. That is not my fault!'

'I am not prepared to discuss it. Nor will I tolerate such impertinence. It is not how young ladies are expected to behave. You will apologize to me for that, and your intemperate language, and you'll send the animal back to Bath. If you do not make arrangements today I will take measures to get rid of him.'

Abby, who had stormed over to the window and was staring down at the carriages in the street below, swung round. 'I apologize if you think I have been impertinent, ma'am, I was trying to explain how it could have happened. But if you force me to send Rusty away I will go with him.'

Lady Padmore opened her mouth to speak, but no words came. Abby took a deep breath, and continued rapidly before she recovered her wits.

'Then maybe without what Mr Wood is paying you, you would have to give up this house and move to somewhere less fashionable. I don't think Caroline would like being in Bloomsbury, wherever that is. She is so excited about her come out, and hoping to meet some eligible young men. I understand in Bloomsbury that would be unlikely, and she would not make an acceptable match.'

This time Lady Padmore managed to speak.

'Don't be so hasty, child. Sit down and let us discuss this calmly. The dog is a nuisance. You cannot spare the time to look after it yourself, so why do you insist on wanting to keep it here?'

Abby crossed the room to the chair indicated. She sensed victory, but managed to keep all hint of triumph out of her voice. She would, she decided, see what pathos would achieve. Her voice became so tremulous she was herself affected by the emotion, and forced tears into her eyes.

'I can take him for walks. You see, he's so fond of me. I rescued Rusty from some boys who were torturing him, when he was just a puppy,' she said, keeping her head lowered and her shoulders drooping. 'He's been with me for three years, and I have trained him to be obedient. He — he is all I have of my own,' she said with a sob, allowing a tear to fall. 'I have no one, and though Aunt Emily has been all that is good to me, I would so like to have had a — a mother, a father, even brothers and sisters!'

She glanced up through her lashes and saw Lady Padmore biting her lip. Abby wiped her eyes with her fingers, forced out another tear, and gave an unladylike sniff.

Lady Padmore heaved a sigh.

'Oh, very well, if the dog means so much to you. I can understand how it must be a comfort, being here amongst strangers. But you must tell that groom of yours to make sure he causes no more trouble, or I shall insist he is sent away.'

Abby blinked hard and managed to squeeze out yet another tear which she allowed to roll down her cheek. 'Oh, thank you! You are being so kind and understanding! I will make sure he doesn't chase any more cats, Lady Padmore.'

Though how she could ensure that, unless Rusty had managed to frighten away all the cats in the area, she did not know.

Lady Padmore waved her away.

'Run along now. The dressmaker is coming later to make up that muslin we bought yesterday for your gowns, and I must go to Keighley House to discuss arrangements for the ball with Lord Keighley.'

★　★　★

The Countess of Wantock put down her coffee cup and sighed.

'I cannot understand why you changed your mind, Julian. I had Jane here again all yesterday afternoon complaining about your selfishness and lack of co-operation and heaven knows what else. You swore you would not let that Padmore woman impose herself and her wretched gal on you, and now you've given her *carte blanche* to turn the house upside down for the next month or more. She'll be here all the time, and you know I find her tedious. She has so little conversation apart from what I can only call malicious gossip.'

'Not *carte blanche*, Mama,' Julian replied, suppressing a smile at the thought of the last little ladybird to whom he had given this. She had been as unlike Lady Padmore as lilies were to turnips. But Abby was no turnip, nor a lily. She was like a bright, glowing rose. He forced his attention back to the matter of the ball. 'She is coming here later this morning, but I will see her and tell her what she may do. With Mr Wood's money she can, she assured me, bring in all the refreshments and hire enough servants to take care of it all.'

'If you permit her to introduce strange servants into the house, then you have lost all your wits. Why, we would find half the silver and ornaments missing, if we were not murdered in our beds.'

Julian laughed, though he was beginning to ask himself what madness had seized him to offer the house to Lady Padmore. Was it just because he had been bewitched by a pair of violet eyes and a mop of flame-coloured curls?

'I wasn't going to permit that. There will be no strange servants, I promise you. Our own people can manage. I'll send for some of the maids and footmen from Wantock House to help.'

His mother frowned.

'And I was thinking I had better go down there to be out of the way for the next few weeks. But no doubt, if you bring all the servants here that will be equally uncomfortable. You'll bring all the cooks too, no doubt.'

'Cousin Hester says she will manage that, and have all the refreshments brought in.'

The countess gave what Julian could only describe as a snort of derision.

'She'll skimp, order the least expensive food, and inferior champagne. I won't have people laugh at us for being cheeseparing. I can see I will have to deal with that. Better still, I'll make Jane help — it's partly her fault — she's quite good at organizing menus. I managed to teach her that, at least.'

'So long as she leaves that brat of hers at home.'

'She will, or he won't be allowed at Wantock House this summer while she goes off to Paris. When is Hester coming?'

'At noon. Mama, I did not mean to involve you. It was a sudden decision, when I saw how disappointed young Caroline was,' he said mendaciously. 'I thought we ought to do our utmost to give the child the best opportunity. Heaven knows, with that mother, she needs all the help she can get to achieve a respectable alliance.'

His mother laughed. 'There is that. I've nothing against the girl, and she can't help her mother. Now, go out somewhere and leave it to me. I don't want you putting Hester's back up, which you're bound to do. You're like your father; he never could abide silly women.'

'Which is why he married you, dearest Mama.'

'Surely all this material will be enough for what I need,' Abby said, as Miss Springer, the dressmaker Lady Padmore had hired, sorted through the bales of silk and muslin. They were in a small room at the top of the house which had been designated the sewing room while she was with them. 'I can have two evening gowns made with these white and blue silks, and I have enough for half-a-dozen new day dresses. Besides, I brought most of my gowns with me.'

Caroline laughed. 'Abby, dear! You don't have a single suitable ball gown. You need some afternoon dresses, a good riding habit, several pelisses and shawls, as well as reticules and shoes and hats and at least one fan. You will probably need new dancing slippers every two or three balls, as they are so thin and get dirty so quickly. Besides, you will want pairs to match every ballgown. You can make do with the nightgowns you have, since you will be buying new ones when you buy your trousseau,' she added, blushing.

Miss Springer smiled.

'She's right, Miss Abby. These I'm to make will do for morning gowns, and to wear at home in the evenings when you don't go out, but you need far more and you'll have to go to a good modiste for those. I can't be expected to make everything myself.'

'I hate shopping! And it's all such a waste of money, as I don't really want to get married. But I suppose I shall have to,' she added gloomily. 'It seems as though there is nothing else for a girl to do, and I suppose Aunt Emily is getting tired of me, and wants her house to herself again.'

'Perhaps she has a beau herself,' Caroline, incurable romantic, suggested. 'I know Mama would like to be married again, but no one has ever shown the slightest interest in her,' she added, giggling.

'I can't see the benefit,' Abby said, as she submitted to being measured by Miss Springer. 'At least if one is a governess or a companion, or even has a shop or runs an inn, one has one's own money and can do what one likes with it. Being married seems to me like slavery. One has to depend on the goodwill of a husband even for money to purchase trifles.'

'Not if one's father or guardian has arranged a good settlement,' Caroline said, and proceeded to instruct Abby on what she ought to insist on as an allowance, and a jointure once her husband died, when the time came for such negotiations.

Abby sighed. 'I seem to have a respectable

fortune,' she said, 'and I wish it could be used to set me up in some sort of business where I could be independent. I would like to breed dogs, but Hartley says that would not be suitable.'

'Of course not,' Caroline said, shocked. 'Well, you might do it when you are much older, if you don't marry. But who is Hartley?'

'He lives next door to us in Bath, and he's my best friend.'

Caroline looked at her with a question in her eye.

'Just a friend? Or does he want to marry you?'

'Good heavens, no! Neither of us wants that. He's been the nearest I have to a brother. We can say what we choose, and we quarrel all the time. I like him tremendously, and we dance well together, but that's all.'

'It seems a great deal to me. I've never had a brother I could be friends with, just girlfriends from school,' Caroline said. 'Dudley is too old, and was never interested in me in any event.' She sighed. 'Oh, let's be more cheerful! That pale green really suits you, Abby.'

Abby looked down at the swath of material Miss Springer was draping round her.

'I always seem to wear green or lemon or

white. I do wish I could wear pinks and reds, like that gorgeous pale pink you bought,' she said. When Miss Springer began rolling up the green muslin she picked up the pink and draped it against herself, looking in the pier glass at her reflection. 'What do you think? It isn't too horrible, is it?'

Miss Springer put her head on one side, considering.

'You know, Miss Abby, it's not at all bad. It's unusual; a striking combination, with your hair, but I really think it would suit you. People with auburn hair never seem to think of wearing pink or red.'

Caroline nodded in agreement.

'It's a pretty colour, and why shouldn't you wear it? Miss Springer, is there enough to make Abby a gown as well as the one for me? I think when we bought it Mama intended to have two gowns made for me.'

They decided there was sufficient material, and Miss Springer promised to make that one the first of Abby's gowns.

'And now we must choose what we are to wear tonight, from our old gowns,' Caroline said. 'We are going to that soirée at Lady Quinton's house. I wonder if any of the patronesses from Almack's will be there? If they are, Abby, we have to make a good impression so that they will give us vouchers.'

'Can't we go to their balls without them?'

'Oh no, they are very strict about whom they admit.'

Abby refrained from saying what she thought about that, and submitted to being dragged down to her room to decide which of the two evening gowns she had brought with her would be more suitable.

★　★　★

The party was at a house in Berkeley Square, the home of Lord and Lady Quinton. Lady Quinton had been one of Lady Padmore's neighbours in Devonshire when she was a girl, though she had been a dozen years older, and she had a daughter the same age as Caroline.

'I'm so thankful Julian has agreed we can have your ball in Grosvenor Square, Caroline,' her mother said, as the carriage took them there. 'It would have been mortifying to come here to Anne's dance, and have nowhere as good to invite them back to yours.'

'Abby's too, Mama.'

'Yes, of course, dear, but Abby knows no one in London.'

'I hope I will know many people by the time of the ball,' Abby said. 'Isn't that why I am here? It isn't to be for several weeks, is it?'

She suspected Lady Padmore regarded her merely as one of the guests at Caroline's ball, rather than an equal debutante, whose ball it also was. She suspected too that Mr Wood was paying rather more than half the expenses, though she could hardly ask Lady Padmore. Young girls, she was realizing, were not supposed to know anything about finance.

She had been rather apprehensive, wondering how Lady Padmore would treat her after their earlier confrontation that morning. But her hostess had been out for most of the day and they did not meet again until dinnertime, when she was all smiles, relating how satisfactory her visit to Grosvenor Square had been.

'The countess has decided to take charge of most of the arrangements, which is very satisfactory, my dears, so all we need to do is plan our gowns and send out the invitations. We must begin to make a list tomorrow, after we have been to order more gowns.'

This evening Abby was wearing the newer of the two evening gowns she had brought from Bath. It was a pale cream in colour, trimmed with deep yellow ribbons slotted through the gathered neckline, and yellow bows on the tiny puff sleeves and round the hem. She carried a gold and green Paisley shawl which belonged to Lady Jordan, but which that lady had insisted she borrow while she was in London.

Caroline was in white, with pale pink embroidery on the bodice and sleeves, and a rouleau of the same shade round the hem. She had confided in Abby that it was one of last year's gowns, which she had worn to local assemblies.

'I wasn't really out, but Mama decided it would help me to become familiar with dancing, so that I shouldn't be too shy here in Town.'

'What happens at these parties?' Abby asked, as the coach drew into Berkeley Square.

'There may be a singer, or a professional musician,' Lady Padmore explained. 'The guests may be asked to perform. Can you play the piano, Abigail? Or sing?'

Abby thought of her lessons in Bath, which Aunt Emily had been so insistent on.

'I play and sing a little,' she said doubtfully, 'but I'm not sure I am good enough to entertain your friends.'

'No matter. If you are asked you must not make a spectacle of yourself by refusing. There is nothing so tedious at these affairs than to have girls pretend to be poor performers, and demand repeated requests before they will oblige.'

'Then I will leap to my feet the moment volunteers are called for. And if people find their ears assaulted by wrong notes and a flat tone it will serve them right!'

Caroline chuckled, but her mother pursed her lips in disapproval. There was no time for her to reprove Abby, however, as the carriage drew up before an imposing doorway and the door was opened by a footman.

There were about thirty people in the large drawing room, where they were shown after greeting their host and hostess at the top of the stairs. A pretty brunette dressed in a white gown similar to Caroline's bore down on them the moment they entered the room.

'Caroline, thank goodness there are girls my own age,' she said, loudly enough for several people nearby to hear.

Lady Padmore frowned, but moved away to greet some of her own friends.

'I'm Anne Quinton, and you must be Abigail Barton. How fortunate you're a redhead. The three of us will look so good together.'

Much as she hated having her hair described as red, Abby had to laugh.

'Call me Abby, please. Do you make your come out this year?'

Anne grimaced. 'Yes, and it's all such a waste, as I mean to marry John Webster, a neighbour of ours. But Mama won't agree to our becoming officially betrothed until after my season. Just because Susannah married when she was seventeen and has come to regret it.'

'Susannah?'

'My sister, She's over there by the window, talking to Julian Wantock. He's her latest flirt.'

'Cousin Julian?' Caroline exclaimed. 'Doesn't her husband mind?'

'He has his own interests,' Anne said. 'Julian only ever flirts with married ladies, then he can't be trapped into marriage. But let's go and sit on that sopha near the other window, and perhaps we won't be asked to perform.'

Taking their hands she towed them across the room. Abby had time to look at Anne's sister and saw a striking brunette, in her mid-twenties, wearing a gown of ruby silk which had what Abby thought was an indecent *décolletage*, and left little of her buxom charms to the imagination.

They were barely seated when Lord and Lady Quinton entered the room, bringing in an elderly, bearded man carrying a violin. Everyone found seats, and the violinist played for half an hour. Abby thought she had never heard anyone else play with such feeling, and she was sorry when he ended, stood up to take his bow, and immediately left the room.

'He's going on somewhere else,' Anne whispered. 'Come with me, we'll slip down the back stairs and get into the dining room while this crowd are making their way down. They are always so slow.'

A buffet supper had been set up, and Anne seized three plates and encouraged her friends to sample all the delicacies. The girls were soon seated at a small table in the library, and a waiter was offering them champagne.

'I always come in here on these evenings,' Anne told them, 'then Mama cannot see I'm drinking more than one glass of champagne. Well, Caroline, are you going to sing for us?'

'I hope not!' Caroline shivered. 'That man was good, and surely amateurs will be a let down after him.'

'No one will care when they have eaten and drunk their fill. Do you play, Abby?'

'Yes, but I'd rather not.'

However, when they all returned to the drawing room and some of the guests were persuaded to play or sing she felt more confident. None of them was particularly brilliant, so when her hostess asked her if she would care to play for a while she readily agreed and took her place on the piano stool.

Most of the earlier performers had brought their own music, and one of the older ladies had accompanied the singers. Lady Padmore had not warned her she might need any music, but fortunately Abby knew many pieces by heart. She decided to sing a simple ballad, 'The West-Country Damosel's Complaint', accompanying herself, and was astonished at the enthusiastic applause which greeted her, and urgent requests for an encore. Lady Quinton was smiling and nodding, so she sat down again and this time, instead of the somewhat melancholy ballad she sang a rousing sea shanty, 'The Rio Grande'.

'You are talented,' Lady Quinton said, and Abby sank down on to a chair close by.

'Congratulations, Miss Barton,' her neighbour said quietly, as the next performer took her seat at the piano.

Abby turned round, smiling her thanks, and looked into Julian Wantock's eyes.

'Thank you, my lord,' she said quietly, and then they had to listen to a vigorous, if somewhat inaccurate rendering of some Haydn sonatas.

'Will you drive out with me tomorrow afternoon?' the earl asked, as they were applauding. 'As your ball is being held in my house I want to get to know you. Besides, you need to be seen in the Park.'

'Do I? Why?'

He blinked. 'Everyone is. You meet half the *ton* there. And I can introduce you to young men who will want to dance with you. My cousin Hester does not have the same extensive acquaintance with suitable bachelors,' he added, and Abby laughed.

'Eligible as husbands, you mean?'

'Isn't that the purpose of the Season?'

'Not mine, I assure you. I don't want a husband, but I suppose I'll have to conform in the end.'

'You may be pleasantly surprised,' he said, laughing.

Abby shrugged. 'I doubt it. What do you drive?' she demanded, and he blinked again.

'Why does it matter? Won't you come with me if you disapprove? Or are you afraid it might be a high-perch phaeton?'

'You really drive one of those?' Abby asked. 'If you do, then of course I will come with you. I've always wanted to drive in one, but none of my acquaintances in Bath is fashionable enough to own one, and Hartley refused to hire one for me, and he wouldn't let me do it for myself.'

'Hartley? Who is he?'

'No one important. He lives next door, and we've been friends all my life.'

'I see. Then I will call for you at four, Miss Barton.'

4

On the following morning Abby was taken to purchase gowns and all the other accessories Lady Padmore insisted were necessary for a girl making her debut.

'This is only a part of what you'll need,' she insisted when Abby queried how much Mr Wood had provided for her new clothing. 'And you need not query the cost, it is none of your business.'

'I'd have thought it was mainly my business,' Abby said.

'Are you accusing me of buying things for myself out of Mr Wood's money?'

'Not at all,' Abby said, though she had wondered how the expenditure on so many items for both girls, lumped together on one bill, could be separated.

'I assume it is coming out of whatever inheritance I am to receive. I think I should be consulted as to whether I prefer to waste some of it now rather than keep the capital intact.'

'Well, I never! What's the world coming to when chits no more than eighteen try to manage their own affairs?'

Belatedly Abby recalled her private vow not to come to cuffs with her hostess again. She knew she was too outspoken, but she would have to curb her tongue if she were to live in amity with Lady Padmore. So she submitted to trying on numerous gowns, and having twice as many as she would have considered ample delivered to Hill Street. They spent the rest of the morning choosing shoes and hats.

By two o'clock Abby was bored to tears, and wondering whether Lady Padmore would ever give them an opportunity to eat. She was also concerned she might not be ready for Lord Wantock when he came to take her driving.

But at last even Lady Padmore was wilting.

'I think we have done enough for today. Tomorrow we will go and visit Mrs Shabner. She makes excellent evening gowns, and we can also order riding habits.'

'I already have one,' Abby said, sighing.

'Perhaps you do, child, but you need one made in London, not by some provincial seamstress.'

Back in Hill Street Abby demolished several slices of ham and cold beef, and a large portion of apple pie.

Lady Padmore eyed her in amusement.

'I hope you will not show such a voracious appetite when we have guests for dinner,' she said, and tittered.

Abby was about to ask if ladies nibbled at their food in public, but had more substantial fare secreted in their rooms, then, recalling her resolution to be tactful, she clamped her lips together.

'It has been a long morning, and I am hungry too,' Caroline said.

'Go and rest now, we are going to the theatre this evening.'

Abby hesitated. She must tell Lady Padmore about the arrangement to drive, but she decided it would be best not to mention it until Lord Wantock was in the house, when it would be difficult for her hostess to object. Somehow she thought Lady Padmore would deny her permission to punish her.

As she went obediently up to her room she pondered on which gown to wear. She had a pale-green walking dress, which went admirably with her darker green spencer, and one of her new hats was a delightful chip straw trimmed with green ribbon bows. The weather was warm, she would not need a pelisse. Her old shoes and gloves would have to do as she had not yet purchased new ones, but they were only last year's, not old at all when she remembered that in the past she had worn most of her clothes until she grew out of them.

At a few minutes to four she went down to

the drawing room, to find two visitors with Lady Padmore. Lady Jane she knew, and the other was introduced as a friend and neighbour in Devon, Mrs Cecilia Croft.

Abby curtsied dutifully, and was about to reply to Lady Padmore's query as to why she had on outdoor clothes when the butler announced Lord Wantock, who came into the room on his heels.

'Good afternoon, ladies. Ah, Miss Barton, I see you are ready for me. Will you excuse us, I don't care to keep my cattle standing? Come, Miss Barton. I'll bring her home safely,' he added over his shoulder, as he steered Abby out of the room.

Abby glanced back and stifled a chuckle. Lady Padmore was glaring at them, while Lady Jane's mouth was slightly open and she had half-risen from her chair.

'I don't think your sister approves,' Abby said, when they were safely out of the house.

'Jane never approves of what I do. But Lady Padmore seemed surprised. Didn't you tell her?' Julian asked.

'No, I didn't have the chance. You see, I thought she might forbid me, but if she didn't know until you were here she could hardly offend you.'

'I like your tactics with Lady Padmore,' he said, grinning, but Abby did not heed him.

She was looking at the high-perch phaeton, drawn by a pair of spirited greys, who were clearly fretting to be on the move, their heads held firmly by an elderly groom. The seat was a good six feet above the ground, and there were small steps to enable the passengers to climb into it.

'Can I help you?' Julian asked.

Abby shook her head.

'I've never driven in one before. I was just working out which foot to use first.'

Without waiting for him to explain she hitched up her skirts and was soon seated, laughing down at him.

'Oh, this is wonderful! May I take the reins for a while?'

Julian scrambled up beside her and hurriedly took hold of the ribbons.

'No, you may not. It's not a lady's carriage,' he said. 'I won't need you, Charles,' he added, and the groom touched his hat and moved smartly out of the way as the earl gave the horses the office.

Abby watched him as he held the greys on a tight rein. They were eager to go, but he kept them at a steady trot as they drove towards the Park. It was glorious being up so high. She had often wished she could ride on the top of a stage-coach, but on the few occasions when they had visited Bristol, or friends of Lady Jordan's who lived in the country near Bath, they had gone sedately in a hired post chaise.

'Will you teach me how to drive?' she asked, as they turned into the Park. 'I've only ever driven a gig before, when we stayed with one of Aunt Emily's friends in the country, and that was so tedious, the pony had only two paces, an amble and a slow trot which he never kept up for more than a minute.'

'You poor girl!' he replied, and Abby hugged herself. He had not refused her request.

The Park was crowded with carriages, riders and walkers. It was the time for the daily promenade, and by now London was fairly full of visitors. The earl nodded at acquaintances, pointing them out to Abby and telling her who they were, but he did not stop to talk to anyone, despite the curious glances that were thrown their way. She supposed they were his friends who were wondering who she was.

'Oh, do look! Who are those frights?' Abby exclaimed, and nodded to where two men were strutting along. 'They can't turn their heads for the high collars, and they must be wearing corsets to have such pinched-in waists. Why do they make such spectacles of themselves?'

Julian laughed. 'Because they want to be looked at.'

'Well, I suppose if they have no natural advantages they have to attract attention by being ridiculous! And who is that enormously fat man in the carriage coming towards us? He's got too many chins to count! The poor horses pulling his carriage must be having a devil of a time.'

The earl stifled a laugh.

'Hush, child! Your voice is too carrying. That is the Prince Regent.'

'Prinny? But Aunt Emily told me he used to be called Florizel, and was handsome!'

'Hush, do, or we'll both be thrown into the Tower!'

Abby gave a peal of laughter, and then blushed as the Prince turned towards them. He bowed as far as his enormous stomach permitted, and then, putting one hand to his lips, blew her a kiss.

'Did you see that?' she gasped, and returned the salute, grinning in delight as the Regent's carriage was borne past them.

'You dreadful child!'

She turned towards him, her expression remorseful.

'Have I committed *lèse-majesté*?' she asked. 'But it seemed only polite to return it.'

Julian was chuckling.

'I just hope Prinny did not recognize me.'

'You know him? Are you one of his Brighton set? Oh, do tell me, is the Pavilion as dreadful as people say?'

'I have met him, of course,' he told her, 'but I am not one of his cronies.'

'No, I suppose you are too young.'

'I would not be in that set whatever age I am!'

'Oh dear, have I offended you? I don't suppose you'll ever teach me to drive now.'

* * *

Julian mopped his forehead as he drove home. While he had been waiting for a footman to emerge and hold the horses Abby had scrambled unaided from the high seat.

'Thank you, that was wonderful,' she called up to him, before turning and running up to the front door.

She could have fallen and hurt herself, he thought, but she seemed agile enough, and apart from revealing rather more of a slender leg than the dowagers would have approved, but which he had appreciated, she had come to no harm.

What a refreshing girl she was, even though some of her comments, if overheard, could have been highly embarrassing. Most of the girls he honoured with invitations to drive with him, if they didn't cringe with fright at the height of the seat in the phaeton, expected to be lifted up and down, with opportunities for close contact. They either flirted outrageously, and then, when he barely noticed them a few days later, sulked, or were so tongue-tied he could scarcely get a complete sentence out of them. None of them blew kisses to the Prince Regent, or mocked overdressed popinjays, or wanted to drive a high perch phaeton, let alone demanding that he teach them how.

He was amused by Abby Barton because she was different, and he was jaded with the average debutante, and could barely recall any of their names. He had been the object of too many ambitious mamas even before he inherited the title, and had learned to be discreet. This, he was well aware, was interpreted by many as pride, but until he met a girl he could spend the rest of his life with he preferred to be thought top lofty. His thoughts returned to Abby. Her outspokenness could easily offend the more straitlaced amongst the dowagers. He frowned. If she acquired a reputation for unconventional behaviour it would harm her chances of making a suitable match. Jane had told him, saying the information had been related to her by Lady Padmore, that her trustees were only able to finance one season for her, so if she failed to catch a husband this year her later opportunities for a good match were questionable. She would probably end up as the wife of a minor country squire. He thought that would be a pity, to have her buried in some country parish, with only genteel neighbours for company.

He suddenly realized that Caroline's fate also hung on Society's acceptance of Abby. If she offended one of the starchy patronesses of Almack's, his cousin would also be denied vouchers. Even if she were not, Lady Padmore could scarcely justify taking her own daughter and not Abby to the weekly balls.

If he tried to warn Abby, would she heed him, or scoff at the rigidity of the code imposed by Sally Jersey and her fellow patronesses? He feared the latter. Somehow vouchers had to be obtained before Abby had opportunities to offend.

Handing over the horses to Charles he made haste to change, and then went to his mother's dressing room. She was pledged to a dinner party that evening, and would be changing.

She welcomed him with a smile, and said she would be ready to talk in a few minutes when her dresser had finished with her hair.

73

He wandered about the room, admiring the many small trinkets, some of them valuable, others mere fairings, which were displayed on most of the flat surfaces. His mother knew and treasured them all, and for each one knew where she had bought it or who had given it to her. In pride of place on her dressing table was a cheap pottery vase which he had bought her when he was seven years old. He had escaped from his tutor and run to the village one afternoon, when his parents were expected back from a visit to friends, a sixpence which he had managed to shake out of his money box clutched in his hand.

A few minutes later the countess dismissed her dresser, and bade him come and sit down.

'What is it, Julian? You look worried. Did you enjoy your drive?'

He grinned at the recollection.

'Mama, do you know who were Abigail Barton's parents? There is some mystery, and I don't think she knows herself.'

'I've no notion, but unlike some people I don't spend my time browsing in the *Peerage*. Why do you ask?'

'I'm convinced she's been brought up a lady, but she's very outspoken, refreshingly so.'

He regaled her with some of Abby's

comments, and though she laughed she was also frowning.

'Almack's?' she said, and he nodded.

'I'm thinking of Caroline too, for if they refuse Abby they are almost certain to refuse Caroline, and that would make life very uncomfortable for both girls. Cousin Hester would blame her, and I already feel that life with her is rather a strain for Abby.'

'I'll be seeing a couple of the patronesses tonight. I'll ask them to tea, and get your Abby to come too.'

'She isn't my Abby,' he protested. 'I just feel sorry for her, and amused by her outspokenness.'

'Yes, dear. Run along now, it's time I was leaving. Are you off to White's for the evening?'

'To begin with. Later we may go on to the East and West, I hear they have a new chef and the food is good.'

*　*　*

Both Caroline and her mother were cool towards Abby that evening. Caroline was hurt she hadn't confided in her about the invitation to ride with the earl and, though she denied it, Abby felt she was also a trifle jealous. Lady Padmore scolded her whenever

75

the servants were not in the room, insisting that in future she not only told that lady of any invitations, whether they be from gentlemen or ladies, or even other debutantes, and ask permission before simply vanishing without so much as a by your leave.

Abby sighed and promised. Then she endured an inquisition on where they had been, what they had talked about, whether they had spoken to anyone else, and whether the earl had suggested taking her up in his phaeton again.

'And the butler tells me it was one of those dangerous highperch affairs. Abby, what would I have said to Lady Jordan and your trustees if you had been hurt? You might have been killed!'

'I wasn't. Lord Wantock is an excellent whip. And he made no promises to take me up again. If he does I shall insist he takes Caroline instead.'

Caroline shuddered.

'I've no desire to ride in one of those dreadful carriages.'

'Very sensible, my dear. I will insist Julian brings his curricle when he takes you driving.'

When, Abby thought, not if, and she suddenly wondered if Lady Padmore hoped to marry Caroline off to the earl. She promised to amuse herself watching that

76

lady's manoeuvres to bring her daughter and cousin together.

Luckily the scolding had to be ended as they went to the theatre. It was a performance of *The Bride of Abydos*, with Edmund Kean, and Abby was absorbed, though she did not much like the actor's blustering style. She had often been to the theatre in Bath, and for a while had nursed an ambition to become an actress, until Mr Wood, when informed, had told her it was impossible.

She decided she no longer wished for this, since most of the people in the theatre paid little attention to what was happening on the stage. How infuriating it must be for the actors to have their best lines unheeded, and only a few of the people close to the stage hearing and appreciating them. Perhaps that was why Mr Kean roared and swaggered so much, in an attempt to be noticed. Besides, Hartley had informed her with irritating male superiority, the actresses were all reputed to be women of light morals. Seeing how some of the men in the boxes opposite ogled them, and how the actresses flirted back, she had no reason to doubt him.

In the first interval two young men appeared in their box. They were, Lady Padmore informed her in an aside, brothers who lived near her country home, the sons of

Mrs Croft, the lady she had met earlier in the day.

'One of them might do for you,' she whispered.

Abby considered them. The elder, Gregory, was attired in very fashionable clothes, not so extreme as the fops she had seen that afternoon, but with shirt points high enough to make it imperative he turned his whole body when speaking to her. His cravat was intricately tied, but she discerned an unevenness and smothered a giggle as she wondered whether he had run out of time or fresh cravats when he had been dressing. He was hung with several fobs, a quizzing glass, wore a number of rings, and carried an over-ornate snuff box which he kept trying, usually unsuccessfully, to open one-handed. He sported more jewellery than most of the ladies, and when she imagined him with ear-rings and necklaces she had to stifle another giggle.

The younger brother, Harold, was plainly, even untidily dressed, and looked sulky. He was plumper than his brother, and would probably become fat as he grew older. She thought of the Regent. She could never imagine him a slender, handsome youth.

'Don't you think this is an utter bore?' Harold asked, while his brother was engaged with Lady Padmore and Caroline.

'The play, or having to visit friends during the intervals?' she asked, and then regretted it as he flushed.

'The whole business of the Season!' he snapped. 'I'd much rather be back in Devon, even if there is no shooting or hunting.'

Unfortunately his raised voice caught the attention of his brother, who frowned at him and said they must be going back to their own box.

'Poor Harold,' Caroline said, after they had gone. 'His brother will get it all, but it's Harold who loves the farm and cares for the estate. I suppose he's been sent to Town to look for an heiress.'

Was she considered a sufficient heiress for an impecunious younger son, Abby wondered, as the next act began? As she didn't know what her fortune consisted of, and when she asked had simply been told it would be sufficient, the unfortunate Harold might have been told to make up to her. She shuddered. When she had occasionally dreamed of a future husband she had imagined someone young and handsome, with impeccable manners and good but not ostentatious clothes, certainly not a boy who was fat and sulky, and lacking in common courtesy. She still believed she did not want to marry, but was coming reluctantly to the conclusion it was the only course open to her.

She paused in her thoughts. Was she unmannerly in her outspokenness? Did she offend in a similar way? She had never before thought of it, but she sat for the rest of the play considering her behaviour, and determined to curb her unruly tongue.

* * *

As she was preoccupied with overseeing the cook in preparation for a dinner party a few days later, Mrs Padmore decreed they could put off more shopping until the following day.

'You can go with my dresser to one of the circulating libraries and take out books to read,' she told the girls at breakfast. 'But do choose something improving, not one of these trashy novels girls seem to like so much.'

'Yes, Mama,' Caroline said obediently, but when she and Abby had escaped from the breakfast parlour she declared her intention of borrowing something interesting, not a boring book of sermons.

The dressmaker was busy making up their gowns, and before they could leave the house she needed to fit those she had already made up in order to check the lengths. It was mid-way through the morning before they reached Bond Street and the circulating library Lady Padmore had stipulated they were to visit.

Abby, who had read widely in Bath, soon chose a book by Maria Edgeworth, an author she liked, and went to sit down while Caroline browsed amongst the shelves. She was content to watch the fashionable crowd, both in the library and the little she could see through the small window of the parade of fashionables passing by outside. She soon realized that the gowns and styles Lady Padmore had selected for them were not as up to date as she had thought, and made a resolution to obtain the most recent copies of *La Belle Assemblée* and insist on the latest styles when they again went shopping.

Was it that Lady Padmore was unaware of changing fashions, or did she not care to be in the mode? As she had selected the same styles for both Caroline and herself, Abby acquitted her of trying to favour her own daughter, and give her a better chance of making a good match.

She was silent on the way back to Hill Street, wondering how best to approach Lady Padmore with her suggestions. She was well aware that lady would resent any criticism of her choice, and Abby could think of no lady amongst the few she had met so far who might be able to help.

They reached home before she had decided on tactics, and found Lady Padmore in the drawing room, entertaining a visitor.

'I am at home on Thursday,' they heard her saying as they approached the door, 'and you would be very welcome to come then, between two and four, Mr Lennox. Is this your first visit to London?'

Abby didn't hear his reply, for she had pushed open the door and flown across the room to fling herself into Hartley Lennox's arms as he rose to greet her.

'Hartley, what on earth are you doing in London?' she demanded as, laughing, he set her down.

'Come to see you, brat. Behave yourself. You're not at home now.'

Abby giggled. 'No, and if I were I would probably be quarrelling with you.'

She suddenly realized how badly she was behaving and turned to apologize to Lady Padmore, only to see the Earl of Wantock looking at her with an expression of disgust on his face.

5

'Are you in love with Mr Lennox?'

Abby shook her head. 'We're friends, that is all.'

She had been sent to her room in disgrace, and had no opportunity of apologizing for her behaviour. Lady Padmore, her expression frozen into a scowl, had refused to listen, and bustled her out of the drawing room where, the doors safely closed, she had told Abby she was an unprincipled, licentious, disgusting trollop. Abby forgot the other adjectives. She was seething with resentment, and immediately she reached her room had dragged out a small valise and begun to pack the few items she would need for a day or so. She would return to Bath. She hated London, and it would serve the Padmore harridan right if she had to give up the Hill Street house and find lodgings somewhere else. Then she discovered she had no money, hid the valise away, and sat down to try to plan how she could obtain sufficient for a ticket on the Mail.

Some time later Caroline, with many furtive glances along the passageway, had crept into her room.

'If you don't love him, why did you kiss him?'

'I didn't! Not kiss him, just gave him a hug. I — well, I was so glad to see him. He's my only real friend, you see. We've been friends ever since I've lived in Bath, at the house next door.'

'He's very good-looking. If you were in love with him I would not be surprised,' Caroline said.

Abby looked at her and saw a wistful smile on her lips.

'Caroline,' she began, thinking that it was odd she of all people was giving Caroline advice, 'Hartley has money, but probably not nearly as much as some of the men we've met here. And it comes from trade. His father and grandfather were merchants in Bristol. His mother moved to Bath when his father died, but there are uncles who carry on the business, and Hartley gets some of the profits. He spends several days a week in Bristol, working with them, and would move there except for his mother, who needs him at home. You'd never be permitted to marry him.'

Caroline blushed. 'I haven't even thought about that. Just because I say a man is handsome there's no need to imagine I want to marry him. Cousin Julian is handsome, but

'I'd hate to be married to him!'

'Why?' Abby demanded, intrigued.

'He always looks at me as though I'm a silly little girl, and he drives dangerous carriages!'

Abby laughed. 'He wouldn't if he loved you. And he's a very good driver. Hartley rarely drives anything but a very safe curricle.'

'Besides, I've decided I don't like living in London. I never know what to say to people. I'd rather live in the country.'

'But don't you want to be married?'

'Yes, and then I wouldn't have to obey Mama all the time. I once thought I might marry Gregory, and live in a small manor house, but I saw last night he's as bad as the rest, and cares only for fashion.'

'What happened after I was sent upstairs?' Abby asked, deciding to change the subject.

Caroline giggled. 'Hartley looked so embarrassed, and kept trying to apologize and explain, but Mama wouldn't let him. Truly, her face was so red I thought she would have a seizure. Cousin Julian sat there looking like a statue, and then he got up suddenly, bowed to Mama, and said he would take Hartley away and introduce him to some friends as he was new to London.'

'Or was he simply removing him to safety?'

'Perhaps. He's known Mama all his life. Then Mama fell into hysterics, and I had to fetch her dresser to help her. Really, I hope I never have to resort to so many remedies! First she had her smelling bottle, then some cordial, and Miss Browne wanted to burn some feathers under her nose, but Mama recalled we had guests for dinner tonight, and the smell would persist, so she went up to her room to rest. That's why I was able to come in here.'

'Am I to come to dinner, or am I in utter disgrace?'

'I don't know, but I heard Mama saying as she went into her room that her numbers would all be upset.'

'If I am banished. She'll have to invite Miss Browne in my place.'

'She'd never do that! Miss Browne is a servant!'

'But a dresser is a very superior one. She always looks down her nose at me when she sees me.'

'I think she might want to leave. I overheard her muttering that this wasn't at all the sort of house she was used to, when she came out of Mama's room.'

'How long has she been with your mother?'

'Only since we came to London. At home Mama makes do with Fanny, but she said she was not used to fashionable life so she left her at home. Fanny was furious.'

Caroline said she had better go, and Abby was left to mixed emotions. She was still furious, but also amused. Her money, she deduced, was paying for the fashionable Miss Browne. Why had the earl taken Hartley under his wing? Why had Hartley come to London? He'd made no mention of coming so soon when she'd last seen him. He'd made an impression on Caroline. She longed to talk to him.

Her musings were interrupted some time later when Miss Browne appeared to remind her to get dressed for the dinner party.

'Lady Padmore expects you in the drawing room in half an hour.'

★ ★ ★

Abby chose to wear one of her new evening gowns, of jonquil silk. She decided that if she were to be chastised by Lady Padmore as a fallen woman she would dress as she pleased, so she added the diamond necklace and ear-bobs. She pulled down the neck of the gown low enough for the diamond to nestle at the edge of the bodice, and threw a silver gauze shawl round her shoulders. Her hair she left loose, so that the curls fell down her back. She twisted one into a ringlet and placed it provocatively over one shoulder. A fan she had bought the previous day, of chicken skin painted with allegorical scenes, completed her attire.

Cautiously she waited by the door of her bedroom, listening through the merest crack. She heard Lady Padmore emerge from her room and go down to the drawing room, followed shortly afterwards by Caroline. Although more than the half hour specified by Miss Browne had elapsed, Abby was determined not to descend until some of the guests had arrived. Though she told herself she did not fear Lady Padmore's anger, she thought it sensible to wait until the presence of guests prevented that lady from further recriminations, and also stopped what her unruly tongue might say if she were again chastised.

Soon she heard new arrivals being conducted to the drawing room, so she gave a final twitch to her shawl, unfurled her fan, and descended.

Lord and Lady Quinton and Anne were seated in the drawing room when she entered. She glanced across at Lady Padmore and frowned when she saw her hostess smiling benevolently at her.

'Come in, my dear. You know my lord and lady, and Anne.'

Abby could see no trace of the anger

previously directed at her, so she shrugged, greeted the guests, and in the bustle of new arrivals went to sit beside Anne and Caroline.

'Why is your mama so friendly?' she asked Caroline under cover of the greetings.

'Hush! I'll tell you later.'

There was no time for more, the conversation grew general, and Abby spent the time considering the men she had not previously met. There was some army captain, a friend, she understood, of the late Lord Padmore, and two of his sons, young men in their early twenties. The last man was a tall, gangling youth introduced as a distant cousin of Lord Padmore's. He was no more than eighteen, and when Abby, feeling sorry for his obvious discomfort, moved to talk to him, he confided that he was currently at Cambridge, and proposed entering the church.

His name was Humphrey, and Abby was not surprised when he was her partner, and they were the last to go down to the dining room, following Anne and Caroline with the captain's sons.

Lady Padmore and the Quintons did their best, but conversation amongst the younger members of the party was at best spasmodic, at worst non-existent. Lady Jordan had drilled Abby with details of the correct dinner table etiquette, and though she dutifully turned away from Humphrey and tried to engage her other neighbour, the captain's older son, in conversation, he responded in monosyllables. Anne, opposite, was having as little success with his brother, and when Abby caught her glance of mute despair she had to bury her face in her napkin to stifle the laughter which threatened to overwhelm her.

When Lady Padmore gave the ladies the signal to leave the room, Abby breathed a sigh of relief. Now she might have an opportunity to talk to Caroline.

Lady Padmore prevented that by ordering Abby to come and sit beside her, with Lady Quinton.

'We are to take tea with the Countess of Wantock tomorrow afternoon,' she said, and Abby thought she almost purred. 'Of course it is mainly to discuss details of Caroline's dance, but she has promised at least one of the patronesses will be there, so, Abby, if you make a good impression, they might give us vouchers.'

Abby groaned inwardly, but managed to hide her annoyance and not reply. It was her dance too, she thought, and she didn't want vouchers for Almack's. But Caroline needed them, especially if she were beginning to have romantic feelings for Hartley. There she would meet more eligible young men, and forget him. He was not likely to be invited. Only young men of birth or fortune were so honoured.

Lady Quinton was speaking, and she forced her attention back to what she was saying.

'So you will permit Caroline and Abigail to attend? I thought Tuesday and Thursday mornings. We will have about twelve couples. Then when they go to Almack's they will all be familiar with the steps of the quadrille, and not too shy to stand up.'

'They used to have dancing parties at Devonshire House, did they not?'

'Oh yes, the duchess began quite a fashion for them. So sensible, I always thought, and determined to do the same for my Anne.'

'Do they teach the waltz at Devonshire House? I'm not sure I want Caroline to dance that, it is so forward.'

'Yes, we must have that, it is permitted now at Almack's, but I give you my word there will be no impropriety. I shall be in the room the entire time.'

Abby was thankful the guests did not stay for long after the men came from the dining room and the tea tray was brought in. As soon as the last guest departed Abby escaped. She had much to think about.

Mr Wood paused before plying the knocker. He had deliberately refrained from visiting Abby until she had time to settle in with Lady Padmore, but he was anxious to know how she did.

When he was shown up to the drawing room he almost laughed. Abby was seated near the window, a piece of embroidery in her hands, and a rebellious expression on her face. She had never, she once told him, wished to hold a needle again, for she either failed to put the silly stitches in the right place or she pricked herself and bled all over the wretched thing.

He half expected her to leap up and throw her arms around him — her normal method of greeting — but, when she remained seated, and after a quick glance at Lady Padmore, similarly occupied in a chair before the fire, merely inclined her head, he decided she was being taught lessons of deportment.

For himself, he was disappointed. Abby's spontaneous affection had always warmed his heart, but he supposed she had now to behave with greater propriety. She wasn't any longer a schoolgirl in Bath, but a young lady making her debut into Society, and she had to behave accordingly. He had a fleeting hope that not all of her liveliness was being repressed. But if she were to make a good marriage, in her odd situation, she had to behave with exemplary care.

Lady Padmore greeted him with, he thought, a slight touch of reserve, but he put it down to her embarrassment because he was paying her, and a suspicion that she was diverting some of these funds to her own benefit over and above the costs of the house.

Abby was well dressed, he noted. Lady Padmore might syphon off some of the money for her own and Caroline's use, but if she could economize and at the same time turn Abby out fashionably, he would not object. She had probably been accustomed to stretching the pounds since her husband died and left her in straightened circumstances.

Supplied with a glass of Madeira, he asked how they went on, whether they had been out much since Abby's arrival, and whether there was anything he could do for them.

Abby looked up and seemed about to speak, but Lady Padmore began to detail all their activities.

'We have to spend a great deal of time shopping,' she said. 'But we are going to my cousin's this afternoon and hope to meet one of the patronesses. I am confident we will be given vouchers. And my cousin Julian is going to have the girls' ball in his own house. I trust I am carrying out your wishes satisfactorily, Mr Wood?'

The last was said with a somewhat belligerent tone, and he raised his eyebrows slightly. Happening to glance at Abby he saw an expression he could not understand on her face. It almost seemed contemptuous. Did she dislike her hostess, or had something occurred to upset her? Then he recalled her often-expressed opinion of Almack's being no more than a marriage mart, and decided she was scornful of the importance her hostess placed on acceptance there.

He had no opportunity for private talk with Abby and, when she asked if she might drive out with him one afternoon, he put her off, saying he kept no carriage and he worked hard in the City most days.

'I will make the time to visit you as often as possible, though I cannot promise when.'

Soon afterwards he rose to leave, and was disappointed when Abby made no attempt to go with him to the door. She bade him a careful farewell, hoping to see him again soon, and he permitted the footman to show him out.

Something, he was sure, was wrong. On his next visit, which he determined would be very soon, he would insist on speaking to her alone.

★   ★   ★

Julian, despite his mother's unconcealed surprise, said he would attend her tea party.

'You know I'm a favourite of Sally's,' he reminded her.

'My dear boy, are you not afraid that if she thinks you have an interest in one of the girls, she will be jealous, and refuse vouchers?'

'Sally isn't vindictive like that. She's more likely to judge that I'll be a more frequent attender than I have been the past two years, and that will please her.'

'I look forward to meeting this Barton child. You say she is lively and unconventional?'

'Most unlike the average debutante. She says exactly what she thinks, no mealy-mouthed comments she thinks people want to hear.'

'Then I hope she can behave conventionally while Sally is here, or she could ruin Caroline's prospects as well as her own. And despite Caroline's deplorable mama I like the child and want to see her respectably established.'

Julian laughed. 'She is well mannered, and

perhaps my presence will restrain her. I confess to being intrigued how she behaves in company, as opposed to being alone with me.'

He caught his mother eyeing him speculatively, and when he went out for a ride early in the afternoon, when the Park was almost deserted, he asked himself what his true interest in Abigail Barton was. She was pretty, but other girls were prettier. She was lively, but many others were too. Where she differed was in her lack of fear, he might almost say lack of respect, and her outspokenness. He found her company refreshing. She would never be dull.

Since inheriting the title, and even before it, he had been put off by the numerous lures cast for him. It had been so obvious his wealth, which was only moderate, and even more his position, attracted all the mamas seeking good matches for their daughters. How would he ever be certain a girl loved him for himself? Occasionally he entertained himself with the notion of the prince who wandered around disguised as a beggar, but he soon laughed at any desire to emulate a man he considered foolish. What sensible girl could even think of becoming betrothed to a beggar!

He surprised himself by thinking Abby might. Then he laughed. Was he considering a girl he had only just met as a possible wife? She would care nothing for his title and position, he decided. Life with her would be full of surprises, never dull.

He got back to Grosvenor Square in time to wash and change and enter the drawing room just as the first visitors were announced. Lady Padmore swept into the drawing room and positively gushed her thanks to her dearest cousin for arranging this wonderful opportunity.

Caroline looked embarrassed and Abby amused. Caroline was demure in white, but Abby was looking enchanting in a pretty rose-coloured gown. He frowned. Surely girls with red hair ought not to wear pink? That was what his last mistress had said. But somehow on Abby the dress looked perfect. The countess greeted them both, and while Julian took the girls across to chairs near the window overlooking the square, began to discuss arrangements for the ball with Lady Padmore.

Half an hour later Julian was beginning to worry. Lady Jersey had not arrived, he was finding conversation with Caroline rather hard going, and only Abby's trenchant comments on the people and equipages passing through the square kept him entertained.

He was listening to a spirited account of Rusty's walk in the Park early that morning, and the yapping objections of a pair of poodles being exercised by a superior footman, who seemed to consider Rusty's presence an affront, when Lady Jersey was finally announced.

She bustled into the room, already speaking, and he let the torrent of words flow over him. There were apologies and explanations of why she had been delayed, enquiries about his mother's and his health, and delight at meeting her dear friend Lady Padmore again, and which of these two enchanting girls was her daughter?

'They call her Silence,' he whispered to Abby, and she had to hide her laughter by hunting in her reticule for a handkerchief.

He recognized his mistake, and prayed Abby would not comment, but she smiled and curtsied gracefully, and the countess was able to ring for tea.

Lady Jersey never seemed to stop talking. She asked numerous questions but rarely waited for the answers. She knew Lady Padmore, and praised Caroline's looks. Then she turned to Abby and congratulated her on defying the dictates of fashion and wearing a colour which actually suited her extremely well.

'Barton? You remind me of someone. Are you related to the Norfolk Bartons? One of them had red hair, I seem to recall.'

'I don't think so, my lady. I'm an orphan, my parents died when I was a few months old, and I have no other relatives. I lived with Lady Jordan in Bath.'

'Emily Jordan? Oh, how long it is since I have seen her. Why did she not bring you out? She is well, I hope?'

'She has not been to London for many years,' Abby said, and Lady Jersey nodded in understanding, and turned to Lady Padmore.

'So you are helping, while Caroline makes her own debut. How very kind of you.'

Julian watched as Abby opened her mouth and then clamped it tight shut. He admired her restraint, and decided she could, when necessary, curb her natural high spirits.

'My husband was a friend of Abigail's trustee, and of Lord Jordan,' Lady Padmore said quickly.

'And you want to find suitable husbands for both of them. I wish you luck, and hope you find two excellent men. I hear Lady Quinton is organizing dancing breakfasts for her daughter, and has invited your charges to join them. Well, I will send vouchers, and I hope to see you all when we start the balls. Perhaps you will honour us as well, Julian?'

she said, turning to him, but before he could reply she rose to her feet and said she really must go, and it had been delightful to meet Caroline and Abigail.

'Whew!' Abby exclaimed, as soon as the door was shut behind her. 'She's like a whirlwind!'

The countess laughed. 'A friendly one. Come here, Abigail, and tell me about yourself. I haven't been to Bath for years, but I remember Lady Jordan. How are you finding life in London?'

'Noisy,' Abby said, as she moved to sit beside the countess. 'But I can endure that if his lordship will teach me to drive his phaeton.'

The countess looked in astonishment at her son, and Julian grinned back at her.

'I think Miss Barton is trying to force a promise from me in front of witnesses. I told you, child, I am never going to teach you to drive my high-perch, nor let you take the reins of my greys.'

She laughed, and he had a sudden urge to take her into his arms. Then he wondered what the devil had got into him. Was she a witch, an enchantress weaving a spell over him?

Fortunately Lady Padmore, with many expressions of gratitude and promises to return soon and discuss the remaining details for the ball, rose to take her departure. Wanting a few minutes to collect his thoughts before facing his mother's quizzical gaze, he elected to accompany them to the door. As he saw them into the carriage he wondered whether he would be considered too old to join Lady Quinton's dancing classes.

6

If they had no other engagements, it had become the custom for Abby and Caroline to walk in the Park each afternoon, taking Rusty with them. On some days Abby also took Rusty to the Park early in the mornings, when it was quiet and she could teach the dog new tricks. He learned quickly, and she delighted to show off his prowess when Caroline and Anne were with her. George had made a strong collar for the dog, and Abby made sure he did not escape and frighten the horses.

The girls kept some distance from the main carriage drive, but were near enough to watch and try to identify the fashionable members of the *ton* as they drove past. Caroline commented mainly on the clothing, especially the hats and bonnets the women wore, but Abby was most interested in the curricles and phaetons driven by the young men, envying them and wondering whether she would ever achieve her ambition to drive her own carriage. When Anne joined them, as she did frequently, she was able to name many of the riders.

'I was in London last Season though I

wasn't out,' she explained. 'And I have met many of them when they have visited Quinton House.'

Abby saw the Earl of Wantock several times, and on each occasion he was accompanied by a different woman. These were invariably beautiful, well dressed, and clearly delighted to be in his company. Abby did her best to discover their names, but Anne knew none of them.

All three girls were there one afternoon, watching Rusty demonstrating his latest accomplishment, when three men approached. Glancing up, Abby saw the Croft brothers and Hartley.

'Hartley!' she exclaimed, nodding to the brothers and drawing Hartley to one side. 'Why haven't you been to see us again?'

He coloured slightly.

'I — there has been so much to see,' he said. 'Remember this is the first time I have been in London on my own.'

'And you wanted to sample the kind of hells your mother would disapprove of! I didn't know you were acquainted with Mr Croft and his brother,' she added.

'Oh, I met them at a club in St James's Square,' he said, and when she chuckled, added, 'and you need not disapprove. It's a perfectly respectable place!'

'How much money did you lose?'

'Only a few — Abby! Why do you assume I was gambling and lost?'

'Didn't you?'

'Not every time! The East and West is very respectable, and has a chef to rival Watier. Many of the men go there mainly for the delicious food.'

'But there is gambling. Don't get addicted,' Abby said, her tone serious. 'One hears of so many people who have been ruined by it, owing thousands!'

'You need not be concerned. I have no great love of faro or cards. It seems to me the banker always wins at faro, and while I enjoy games of skill, card games which depend wholly on chance do not attract me.'

Before she could respond Anne came across to join them.

'Abby, Caroline tells me Mr Lennox is a friend of yours from Bath.'

Abby introduced them, and Anne smiled at him.

'Will you join our dancing parties, Mr Lennox? I have persuaded Gregory and Harold to come.'

'Dancing parties? You mean balls?'

Anne laughed. 'No. They take place in the mornings, and we have breakfast afterwards. My mama holds them on Tuesdays and Thursdays, and they are mainly designed to teach us the moves for the cotillion, and even the waltz, so that we don't disgrace ourselves at Almack's. Do say you'll come. We live in Berkeley Square; Gregory will show you.'

Hartley cast a swift glance towards Caroline, then nodded.

'Thank you, I'll be delighted.'

The young men then escorted them back to Hill Street, and Abby was amused to see how quickly Hartley went to walk beside Caroline, and how prettily Caroline blushed as she looked up at him.

It was with some reluctance they parted. Anne was to await her mother's maid, to escort her home, but the men were scarcely out of earshot before she was congratulating herself on recruiting them.

'Mama was finding it difficult to persuade enough men to join,' she said. She has even asked the Earl of Wantock, though he is an excellent dancer. But she told him he could take the lead and show us all what to do.'

★　★　★

To Abby's surprise Mr Wood appeared a few days later, driving one of the newly fashionable cabriolets, and invited her to drive with him.

She was delighted, and soon they were heading for the Park, a diminutive grizzled tiger riding on the dummy board.

'It almost sits on the ground!' Abby exclaimed. 'If we meet anyone driving a high perch we won't be able to shake hands, they will be so far above us.'

'I'm not disposed to approve of high-perch phaetons, unless the drivers are competent. Too many are driven by boys aping Corinthians, and they create accidents, to themselves and others.'

'But a cabriolet is very fashionable,' Abby said consolingly, 'and I'm sure it needs a great deal of skill to control,' she added, as they swept through the gates in great style, overtaking a curricle driven by an elderly lady with inches to spare.

'Baggage!'

She chuckled. 'I didn't know you drove any type of carriage.'

'I used to, in my far-distant youth, before I became so immersed in business affairs.'

She frowned up at him.

'I've never understood what your business is. I know you have an office near the Royal Exchange, and I think you are what they call a stock jobber?'

'I deal on the stock market, yes, for myself only, but I am not a jobber dealing for others.

I also import and export a variety of goods, and have various other interests.'

'I heard someone the other day complaining because he said stock jobbers were not allowed to have other businesses.'

'A few are, where they are long-established businesses.'

'How did you become my trustee?' she asked. 'You must have known my parents?'

'Indeed. You were left in my care.'

'Then won't you tell me who my mother was, and whether I have any relatives in her family?'

'I was asked not to, by your mother, who wanted nothing more to do with the family which cast her out. I do understand why you want to know, Abby dear, but I cannot break my word to her. After we have made a circle of the Park and I have demonstrated my ability with the ribbons, shall we go and eat ices at Gunter's? The day is hotter than usual at this time of year.'

Some time later they were in Berkeley Square, and the tiger was sent across to the famous confectioner's, while Abby and Mr Wood sat under the maples, just beginning to show a hint of green.

A waiter brought out the ices and, as they ate, Mr Wood asked Abby if she were content with Lady Padmore.

Abby considered the question as she licked the spoon.

'She is buying me far too many clothes, more than I consider essential. She is introducing me to important people. She has acquired vouchers for Almack's, which I am told can make or ruin a girl's chances. If I have to spend the Season in London, then I am content with her. Caroline is friendly.'

'You don't sound very enthusiastic.'

'In some ways I am enjoying a new experience, but I think a good deal of the time is wasted on trivial entertainments. I understand I can have only this one Season, and that I am expected to attach a husband, so I will do my best.'

'Only one Season? Who told you that?'

'I forget. Either Lady Padmore or Caroline. But as one is more than enough for me, I quite see I have to make an effort to find someone I could be content with.'

'I hope you will be much more than merely content! Abby, you can have as many Seasons as you wish, there is plenty of money, so please only marry someone you can love.'

'If there is money, could I not have it to set myself up in some business? I really would be far more content running an inn, or a shop,' she replied, refraining from mentioning her real preference, somewhere she could breed dogs. If Mr Wood showed any interest in this notion of a business, she would mention it later. One step at a time, she cautioned herself.

★ ★ ★

On the following morning Caroline and Abby went to the first dance breakfast. As well as the lessons she had had, Abby had attended a few private balls in Bath, and once or twice been to the Assembly Rooms there, and was confident she knew most of the steps, but Caroline confessed she knew very little, apart from a few country dances.

Anne greeted them and took them through to the large ballroom.

'It's cold in here, with just a dozen or so of us, but Mama says we can move into the music room if we wish. We have to have a pianoforte.'

Abby was looking round, wondering who might be there, but she knew no one. There were two young men and half-a-dozen girls, and Anne made haste to introduce them. Some were schoolfriends, others the daughters of Lady Quinton's friends. Of the men, one was a cousin, the other a brother of one of the girls. Neither of these two looked particularly pleased to be there.

After a few minutes of stilted conversation, Hartley and the Croft brothers came in and, hard on their heels, the Earl of Wantock. Lady Quinton followed him in, and after her came a small lady carrying sheets of music.

'Well, my dears, I think that is all of us. Now, will you be too cold here, or should we move into the music room? There won't be so much space there, but we could manage.'

They all looked round, no one being willing to speak first, until Abby took a deep breath.

'If we are dancing, ma'am, we should keep warm,' she said.

'Then let's begin,' Anne said, and shivered slightly.

'Good. Let us try the cotillion. How many of you have danced it before? My lord, I know you are an expert, and Anne has danced it, so will you lead one set? Who else?'

As there were several young people who admitted enough knowledge to lead, three sets were formed, and they were soon ready. The pianist found the right music, and they began, with Lady Quinton calling out the figures.

For a while, as the earl and Anne performed the opening steps, all went well. They bowed to partners and corners, everyone else following, and managed a balance and a half promenade. Then a ladies' chain was called, and none of the girls apart from Anne in one set, and Abby in the other, knew what to do. Some girls followed them, others went in the opposite direction, and one stood quite still, not venturing either way.

They collapsed into laughter, and congratulated themselves they had not been at a public ball. After half an hour, they were all able to go through the simpler movements, and Lady Quinton called a halt.

'Now for a waltz, though you must remember, girls, you must not perform this in public until one of the patronesses has given permission. They are ready to do this if they see you are behaving modestly, so you need to know the steps. My lord, you must be expert, so will you demonstrate with Anne?'

From what she had heard from some of the other girls, Abby knew they could dance the waltz, and she knew the steps herself. Was Lady Quinton simply choosing dancers she was sure could perform the steps, to demonstrate, or did she contrive that Anne and the earl should be partners because she hoped for an alliance between him and her daughter?

It would, Abby decided, be a very suitable match. Both families, as far as she knew, were old and respected. Both appeared to be wealthy, had big town houses and country estates. The earl was ten years older than Anne, a gap in years she had always understood was an appropriate one. And they made a handsome couple.

After a short demonstration the earl and Anne took different partners, those who admitted they had never before attempted to waltz. Lady Quinton paired off the others, trying to match the more experienced with the less able. Abby was paired with Harold, and she discovered he had no sense of rhythm, and clutched her to him much too closely for comfort, since it caused him to tread on her feet more than once. Besides, he had splashed on some rather pungent scent, and after a while she tried to breathe through her mouth. Soon, she hoped, they might be able to change partners.

This did not happen, for Lady Quinton declared they had done enough for one morning, and it would be folly to attempt to learn too much too quickly.

'Breakfast is ready, my dears,' she said, and asked Anne and the earl to lead the way to the dining room.

Abby lingered, going over to the pianist and thanking her for her playing.

The woman smiled. 'A pleasure, my dear.

You are already a good dancer. I know these tunes so well I was able to watch you all. Now I must get back to my real work, and Lady Quinton is waiting for you.'

Abby found Hartley waiting for her as well, and they went to the dining room.

'Who is the pianist, Lady Quinton?' Abby asked. 'She played very well.'

'She is my dresser, but her father was a musician, a teacher, so she has played all her life. It is very convenient to have her accompany us, and she enjoys the opportunity. One day you must come and listen to her playing more advanced pieces. I think she might have made a career of it if she had been given greater confidence, but she is normally very retiring.'

In the dining room most of the dancers were seated round the long table, but the earl was acting as butler, helping the girls as they selected items from the extensive buffet. He smiled at Abby, and when she and Hartley had helped themselves to ham, eggs and kidneys, he followed them and took a seat next to Abby.

'I'm sorry we had no opportunity of dancing together,' he said. 'You appear to know the steps.'

'Lady Jordan sent me to dancing lessons,' she replied. 'This ham is excellent. Do tell me, are you going to marry Anne?'

He was just taking a sip of coffee, and at these words he almost choked.

'My dear girl,' he managed, as soon as he could speak again, 'you should not ask those sort of questions.'

'Oh dear, have I offended you? It was just that Lady Quinton seemed to pair you with Anne all the time, and I wondered whether you were betrothed, or she was trying to push Anne, literally, into your arms.'

'We are not betrothed. I am promised to no one. I have had countless debutantes set their caps at me, and fond mamas who have done their best to interest me in their daughters. And you need not look at me as though I were a great coxcomb!' he added. 'I am quite aware it is my title and fortune which attracts them, rather than my person!'

Abby grinned at him.

'I think you are handsome apart from your title and fortune,' she said, and he almost choked again as he laughed.

'Shall we talk of something less personal? How is that dog of yours? Have you taught it any more tricks?'

'I try, in the mornings, when there are few people in the Park to interrupt. Rusty is clever, but he needs to concentrate, not be interrupted. Oh, I think we are being told we should be finishing. Lady Quinton is looking rather pointedly at the clock.'

* * *

The earl, despite a late night at the tables, rose early the following morning and took his horse to the Park. He was more and more intrigued by Abigail Barton, and her frank outspokenness. Perhaps she would be in the Park with her dog, and he could talk more to her.

He was to be disappointed. She was there, but so was the fellow from Bath who seemed to know her very well indeed. What was his name? Hartley something.

He was just deciding to retreat when Abby saw him and waved. He rode over and dismounted to talk to them.

'Mr Lennox,' he said, recalling Hartley's name just in time, 'did you find the dancing at Lady Quinton's of value?'

'It was interesting, and as Abby insists I cannot dance as well as some other people we meet in Bath, I hope to improve my performance. You have no need of instruction, though.'

The earl nodded.

'I was invited as an expert,' he said. 'It indicates I have occupied my time rather frivolously.'

'But Caroline says you were in the army, fought at Waterloo, and much of the time in Spain,' Abby said. 'That is not being frivolous. Hartley wanted to join, didn't you?'

Hartley nodded. 'I wished to purchase my colours when I came of age a few months ago, but I am an only son, and my uncles have no sons to take over the business. Besides, I really had no wish to go to India.'

'You might have come back a Nabob,' Abby said. 'And I thought your uncles had daughters. Why could they not manage the business?'

'Women can't manage complicated concerns like ours,' Hartley told her. 'In any event, they will get married soon, no doubt.'

'Women can manage just as well as men. Look at the women who control huge households, or run schools, and do it without making a great to do about it. If I had an opportunity to manage a large business like yours, I would prefer that to marriage.'

'Or breeding pugs!' Hartley said. 'That is hardly the same.'

'Breeding pugs?' the earl said, deciding it was time to intervene in what he suspected was a frequent cause of dispute.

It appeared Hartley knew Abby very well, and from their behaviour he deduced they were like brother and sister, with no romantic

116

feelings towards one another. He considered that fortunate. If they married Hartley would soon find Abby attempting to run his business. He smiled at the thought, but was sure she would run it well.

'That's what Abby wants to do,' Hartley told him.

'Not pugs! I prefer useful dogs.'

'Like Rusty?'

He bent to pat the dog, who had been sitting beside Abby, turning his head towards each speaker in turn. Rusty held out a paw, and the earl laughed and shook hands.

'What a polite animal. What breed is he?'

Abby cast a swift glance at Hartley, and then burst out laughing.

'Hartley says I make it up depending on who asks. Let me see. You are clearly aristocratic, so what dogs are favoured by the *ton*? But you can't have lapdogs! It's a pity he has no spots, so he can't be one of those carriage dogs, Dalmatians. I suggest a mixture of poodle, spaniel, Baluchi hound, Irish wolfhound and Italian greyhound.'

'You see? She is incorrigible.'

'And I am going to be late for breakfast!' Abby said. 'Will you both be going to Lady Quinton's tomorrow?'

Without waiting for them to answer she turned and began to run towards the entrance, Rusty leaping joyfully at her side. The earl burst out laughing.

'Mr Lennox, come home with me and join me for breakfast. What is this business of yours that Abby thinks she could manage?'

* * *

Lady Padmore, having quizzed the girls about which men had been present at the dance breakfast, decided they needed more gowns and new dancing slippers, so the rest of the morning was spent shopping. When they returned to Hill Street it was to find the footman struggling to carry a trunk upstairs, and the hall cluttered with various items of luggage.

'What is this?' Lady Padmore demanded. 'I have invited no guests to visit.'

'I'm not a guest, Mama, and surely you won't turn me away.'

A tall, willowy young man emerged from the dining room, lounging against the door jamb. He was handsome in an effeminate way, his hair as blond as Caroline's, very artfully disarranged. He was dressed in regimentals, but Abby thought he might have difficulty actually fighting, for his breeches clung to his rather thin limbs, and the waist of his coat was tightly pinched in, while his

118

cravat was tied in a manner she had never before seen on a military man.

Lady Padmore was holding out one hand to him, and had the other over her mouth.

'Dudley! My son! Oh, I shall swoon with joy! I did not think to see you for months!'

Caroline merely nodded to her brother, and somewhat acerbically suggested they might all go into the dining room and sit down, if Dudley could remove himself from the doorway. He smiled at her languidly and did so, and Caroline assisted Lady Padmore into the room and helped her to a chair. A nuncheon of cold meat, fruit and jellies had been set on the table, and Abby saw that Dudley had already begun, and had drunk at least half a bottle of claret.

'Why are you here?' Lady Padmore demanded. 'I thought your regiment was about to go to some outlandish place.'

'It was, so I have sold out. I have had enough of army life, so I decided to come and see how things were in Town.'

'Sold out? When you plagued Mama for over a year until she found the money to buy your commission!' Caroline exclaimed. 'I hope you intend giving her the money back.'

'Caroline, dear, I'm just thankful to see my boy home. I never did like the idea of him being involved in battles.'

'What do you think the army do? They don't all strut about guarding the Prince Regent. If Dudley wanted just to preen in fancy dress he should have chosen a different regiment!'

'They cost too much, if you recall, little sister! Mama insisted on keeping some money for you, so that you could catch a husband and be off her hands. Have you done so yet?'

'Children, you are not in the nursery now. Dudley, I must introduce dear Abigail, who is doing the Season with Caroline.'

Abby inclined her head, and ate quickly. She would prefer to leave the family alone to quarrel without her being a witness. Lady Padmore did not protest when she excused herself to retreat to her room.

The hall was by now free of Dudley's luggage, and she ran up to her room, where she got out her writing case and started a letter to Lady Jordan. If Dudley were to remain here, and it seemed most likely, the atmosphere promised to become unpleasant. How she longed to go home to Bath.

She finished the letter and went downstairs to place it on the hall table for the footman to take to the post. As she was returning to her room, trying to decide what to wear for their visit to the theatre, Dudley emerged from the drawing room and before she could evade him had backed her into a corner.

'Abigail, the heiress,' he said, leaning over her. 'I understand it is thanks to you and your money that Mama and Caroline have hired this house. I am most grateful to you.'

'To my trustees, who arranged it, sir.'

'Of course.'

He swayed slightly, and she detected the wine on his breath. She moved to try and pass him, but he stretched out his arm and barred her way.

'Don't be shy, my pretty. I have to thank you.'

Before she could avoid it he grasped her by the shoulders and pulled her close, then aimed a slobbering kiss at her lips. Abby twisted her head aside and wrenched away from him, then swung her arm and delivered a stinging blow to his cheek. He glared at her, astonished, as he put his hand to his reddening face.

'If you even touch me in future, I will take myself and my fortune away from this house, and you will see your mother and sister living elsewhere,' she threatened, and before he could reply ran up the next flight of stairs to her room.

7

The earl and Hartley breakfasted in a small room at the back of the house, and while the footman was there chatted about the Quinton dance breakfast. Having satisfied their hunger with several slices of beef, rolls with fresh butter, and some coddled eggs, they went to the earl's study where Julian gestured to a chair one side of the fireplace.

'Sit there, and tell me about Bath. You live next door to Miss Barton, I understand. She's a very pretty girl.'

'I suppose she is, but I've known her since we were children. I've never really considered it. Normally I don't like redheads, they have freckles. I prefer blondes.'

The earl glanced at him from beneath lowered lashes. He'd said normally. Did that mean he liked Abby? Enough to want to marry her?

'Is there some special blonde down in Bath?'

Hartley flushed slightly. 'Oh no, I haven't been much in the petticoat line.'

'So you didn't come to London in search of a wife?'

'I came because a few months ago I inherited some money my father left, and I've never been here since I was a child.'

'Then we must show you around. Have you met many people yet?'

'Just the ones at Lady Quinton's, plus a couple of fellows at my hotel. Miss Padmore is your cousin, I believe?'

'In some way, but distantly. Miss Barton is staying with her and Lady Padmore is bringing her out.'

'At the same time as her own daughter, I understand. Tell me, I am such an ignoramus, how are girls brought out, as they say?'

The earl laughed. 'It's a ritual. They attend as many parties as they can during the Season, as many as they have the stamina for. Popular young ladies may attend three or four in a night.'

'So one can never be sure of finding them at any one party? Why are there so many arranged for the same time?'

'The Season is short, three months or so.'

'And then in June or July I believe everyone goes to Brighton. Will Lady Padmore be taking Abby and Miss Padmore there?'

'I really don't know. I expect she is hoping to find husbands for them before then.'

'At these parties.'

'There they are supposed to meet eligible

123

young bachelors, and when one shows an interest in a girl their parents or guardians assess his suitability, fortune and rank, and his family assess hers.'

'It sounds like a market.'

'It is.'

'And if the man is not rich enough I suppose the girl is made to reject him. Do all these girls want a title?'

'It helps,' the earl said, and frowned. 'I suspect most of the lures I've had cast at me are due to my title.'

'Then a man without a title is handi-capped. Is Lady Padmore hoping to secure a title for her daughter?'

'She's hoping to secure mine!'

'Yours? Does Miss Padmore want a title?'

'I can acquit Caroline of that. And she is not interested in me. But the real market is at Almack's.'

'I've heard of that. Do Abby and Car — Miss Padmore go there?'

'They've been given vouchers. Would you care to go? It's far from exciting, I warn you.'

'Would they admit me? I come from merchant stock.'

'Don't sound so despondent. If Sally Jersey approves of you, I can take you as my guest. I'll find out where she will be during the next week, and contrive to introduce you.'

It was puzzling, the earl thought later, as he bade his guest farewell. Had Hartley followed Abby to London? Were his remarks about preferring blondes meant to throw him off the scent? Marrying a merchant would be considered far more suitable for Abby, with her unknown background, than what her guardians clearly expected, for her to make a grand match with someone from the *ton*.

★ ★ ★

There were two more dance breakfasts at Quinton House before the opening ball of the Season at Almack's, and Julian became more and more frustrated.

Lady Quinton ruled, deciding which dances, and pairing the more experienced with those who needed practice. She was not blatant about it, but after the first time Julian began to be suspicious. He was only rarely asked to dance with Anne, but she was almost always in the same set, and Abby never was. Indeed, most of the time Abby was placed in the third set, furthest away from him, with Lady Quinton smilingly complimenting her and suggesting she could lead the others.

The only chance he had to talk to Abby was afterwards, when they were at breakfast. And on the second occasion even that brief contact was denied him, since Lady Quinton demanded his opinion on the propriety of allowing Anne to visit Vauxhall Gardens when they opened in May, and hinting strongly that if he were of the party she would have fewer qualms.

Was she angling for a match between himself and Anne? It would, he admitted, be appropriate, for the families had been friends for two generations. Their fortunes were comparable, it was time he thought about marriage, and Anne was a pleasant, friendly and intelligent girl who would make an admirable wife. He just didn't want her. Did he want Abby?

After the second Tuesday breakfast he had his horse saddled and rode out to Richmond. He had some serious thinking to do and needed to be alone. The girl intrigued him. She was so unlike the average debutante with her outspoken ways and her lack of interest in the topics which seemed to fill the minds of other girls her age. He knew nothing of her background, who her parents had been, whether, in fact, they had been respectable. There were rumours they had eloped to Gretna, but no definite information. She was believed to have a competence but, unusually, no one appeared to know precisely how much.

He cared nought for her ancestry, but he was well aware most of his family would throw up their hands in horror at the very notion of his marrying a nobody, as they would call her. He did not need a fortune. His own, though not comparable with some, was adequate to keep up Wantock House and his other properties. His sister was married, and he had no other siblings to provide for. He could please himself.

Riding back to London late that afternoon he had decided nothing. He would see Abby the following night at Almack's, and Lady Quinton would not be able to prevent him from dancing with her, though there was not likely to be any opportunity of holding her in his arms during a waltz. None of the patronesses would sanction that until they had seen how the debutantes comported themselves.

Would his mother like Abby, and accept her into the family? The countess was far from high in the instep, and had friends, mainly blue stocking ladies, who were not a part of the *ton*, or only on the fringes. She would never be less than welcoming to whatever wife he chose, but there was a great difference between polite acceptance and friendly welcome.

Passing the Hyde Park turnpike he began

to wonder if he should ask his mother's advice, then he laughed aloud. He was eight and twenty, a seasoned soldier, head of an important family, owner of considerable estates which he supervised with success. He did not need his mother's approval in the choice of a wife. The plain fact was, he had never before seen any girl he had even considered asking to marry him.

Tomorrow he would dance with her, and make every opportunity he could for getting to know her. He shook his head. He was deceiving himself. He did not need time, he knew he wanted her.

★ ★ ★

Abby was amused at the trepidation with which Caroline anticipated her first visit to Almack's.

'It's just another club, for dancing,' she said, but Caroline shook her head in denial.

'It's not just any assembly,' she said. 'If a girl offends the patronesses, or doesn't take, it can ruin all her chances of a good match.'

'That's nonsense, one can meet suitable men at other places.'

Despite herself, she was not quite so blasé as they approached the club. Lady Padmore had fussed all day about what the two girls would wear, and they had been forced to parade before her in different gowns so that she could decide which was the most appropriate. In the end Caroline was told to wear white, which Abby thought made her look insipid, while she was permitted, after considerable argument, to wear pale blue.

Caroline's was a new gown, muslin with silver thread embroidery over the bodice, and not a shred of colour otherwise. The neckline and edges of the sleeves were ruffled, and the hem was lightly scalloped with an edging of silver lace. Lady Padmore decreed she would wear with it a single strand of pearls, and with long white gloves and her fair hair arranged in a knot on her neck Abby thought she looked like a ghost, she was so pale. She longed to use some rouge to brighten Caroline's cheeks, but knew this would not be permitted, even if she had any. Lady Padmore possessed some, she was sure, for that lady's high colour did not always seem natural, but she would never admit to it.

Abby's gown was of blue watered silk, and she wore it despite Lady Padmore's predictions that she would be thought fast.

'Young girls always wear white, especially on their first appearances in Society,' she insisted.

'My white ballgown is almost the same as Caroline's,' Abby pointed out. 'It would surely be preferable for us to look different.'

She didn't need to say that with her own more vibrant colouring the contrast with Caroline would be cruel. Lady Padmore understood, gave way, and they set out for Almack's. The outside of the building, in King Street, was plain. They ascended the steps and after leaving their wraps entered the ballroom. Abby expected something elaborate, because of all she had heard about it, and the reverence with which it was treated, but she was most disappointed. The room was plain, a long space broken by tall windows surmounted by arches, and the walls simply decorated in panels and unpretentious draperies.

The men all wore old-fashioned knee breeches and white cravats, and Abby had heard they would not be admitted dressed otherwise. She glanced round, hoping to see some people she knew, but all were strangers apart from Lady Jersey, who stood near the doorway talking to two other ladies. Lady Jersey glanced at her and smiled vaguely. Abby was sure she didn't remember who she was, but when the music started for a country dance Lady Jersey came across the room with two abashed-looking young men in tow, and introduced them to Abby and Caroline as suitable partners.

Halfway through the dance Abby saw the Earl of Wantock enter the room. She caught her breath and almost missed her move. In the formal wear he looked more handsome than ever.

When her partner returned her to where Lady Padmore was sitting, she hoped the earl would come to speak to her, and perhaps even dance with her, but he remained at the far side of the room, and while he danced with Anne Quinton she was claimed for the first cotillion by another partner introduced by one of the other patronesses, she did not know who.

The next dance was a waltz, and Abby sat beside Lady Padmore, feeling rebellious, especially when she saw the earl dancing with a ravishing dark-haired beauty a few years older than herself.

'It's so stupid, not permitting us to waltz,' she muttered to Caroline. 'Who is that the earl is dancing with?'

Caroline chuckled. 'I have no notion. Are you jealous, Abby? I'm sure he will come and dance with you soon. At Quinton House he could barely take his eyes from you.'

Abby disclaimed, but could not resist a smile of satisfaction some time later as the earl approached when a country dance began.

'Miss Barton, may we dance?'

Abby's hand trembled in his as he led her on to the floor, and she took a deep breath. What was the matter with her?

She soon discovered that the movements of the dance prevented them from enjoying proper conversation. After just a few words they had to separate, and Abby sensed that the earl was as frustrated as she was herself to have sentences cut off in the middle, and then have to make polite noises to a new partner.

At the end of the dance, though, she discovered it was eleven o'clock, the doors were shut against latecomers, and supper was to be served.

'Don't expect a feast,' the earl warned, as he led Abby towards the supper room and found a small table for them. 'You may have tea, orgeat or lemonade. The patronesses insist on gentility, and refuse to contemplate wine for fear we will all get inebriated and the ball will degenerate into bacchanalia.'

'That seems unlikely. Whatever you men do when at your clubs, you all behave with boring propriety when in mixed company. Well, most do,' she added, thinking of Dudley.

'When have you encountered bad behaviour?'

He sounded fierce. Abby decided not to tell

him about Dudley's kiss.

'He was just pompous and unpleasant to his mama. Rude and surly.'

'Would you have that sort of behaviour in general?'

'Not bacchanalia, of course, but their conversation is usually so dull and predictable.'

The food was, Abby found, quite unappetizing, nothing like the elaborate confections she had so far enjoyed at the few parties she had attended. But after several hours of energetic country dances and cotillions she was hungry, and ate the thinly-sliced bread and butter and plain cake, and drank the lemonade.

'Keep a cotillion for me,' the earl said, as they returned to the ballroom. 'I'm sorry it cannot be a waltz, but soon I will persuade Sally or Lady Cowper to give you permission, and then I want to have the first waltz with you.'

They said no more, having reached the chair where Lady Padmore was sitting. The earl bowed to them both and departed. Lady Padmore looked after him speculatively.

'Tell me, child, about these dance breakfasts. I heard my cousin Julian attends. Has he danced with you there?'

'Oh, no, because in general Lady Quinton

pairs those of us who know the steps with partners who do not.'

'Has he danced with Caroline?'

'Once or twice, I believe,' Abby said, glancing at her. Was she eager to capture the earl for Caroline? 'He has danced with Anne quite frequently,' she said, and watched in amusement as Lady Padmore pursed her lips.

The cotillion was a little more satisfactory than the country dance, Abby discovered. There was time for brief conversations as they stood watching the other couples dance the various steps.

'Will you drive out with me tomorrow?' the earl asked as the dance neared its end.

'In your phaeton?' Abby asked, and he grinned at her.

'If I said not, would you refuse?'

'Of course! But I know you won't disappoint me.'

★ ★ ★

Neither of the girls rose early the following day. They had been very late getting home, and it was noon before they woke. Lady Padmore was still in her room, having said she did not wish to be disturbed until she rang. They were sitting in the breakfast parlour, comparing impressions about Almack's, when Anne came in.

'That was wonderful,' she sighed, after accepting a cup of chocolate. 'I danced every dance, except for the waltzes, and Mama says I will probably be permitted to dance those next week. Did you dance twice with anyone, Caroline? I saw you dancing with Julian Wantock, Abby. Mama was furious because he only danced once with me, and you danced with him twice. But I've had quite enough dancing with him at the breakfasts.'

'Why? Don't you like him?'

'Not as much as you do, Abby! He's boring. He's not at all interested in fashion, or gossip. He'd rather talk about politics.'

'He always seems to be dressed fashionably,' Abby said, 'and gossip can be boring if you don't know the people.'

'I suppose so. But Mama thinks she can catch him for me, and I haven't the least desire to marry him. What about you, Caroline? He danced with you last night, and I overheard your mama saying what a well-matched couple you made.'

Caroline shook her head.

'I'm always nervous when he talks to me, I don't understand half what he says. And I utterly refuse to go driving with him in that dangerous phaeton of his.'

'But it's exciting!' Abby exclaimed. 'I wish

he'd teach me to drive it.'

Anne stared at her, then smiled.

'He much prefers you to either of us. I noticed how he always tried to sit beside you at the breakfasts. When are you going driving with him again?'

'Well, today, this afternoon.'

'Does Mama know? She was furious last time because you did not ask permission,' Caroline said.

'I told her on the way home, but she was half asleep, I don't know if she heard me.'

Caroline laughed. 'I'll tell her I heard you.'

'He hardly ever drives a girl twice,' Anne said. 'Mama says he is afraid of the gossip. He's such a good catch, he's had girls making up to him ever since he came of age, but even more so when he inherited the title so young. So you are honoured, Abby. Perhaps he'll offer for you.'

Abby shook her head.

'I think he is just amused by me. He is always laughing at the things I say.'

Soon afterwards she escaped to her room, and sat with her chin in her hands, thinking back to every conversation she had ever had with the earl. He did like her, she was sure, but that did not mean he would ever offer for her. She sighed. He was just the kind of man she could envisage being married to, but the very idea of him considering her as a wife was nonsense. He would marry someone well connected, but she was a nameless nobody.

* * *

The earl was puzzled. Abby, when he drove her to the Park, was uncharacteristically silent, responding to his overtures in monosyllables. Normally when they talked she had favoured him with her impressions of the people she had met, or, as on the other occasion, those they encountered. He had expected her to be full of amusing observations about the people she had met the previous night. Perhaps she was tired, he thought. The dancing at Almack's went on late, and she was probably unused to such hours. He had devoted a great deal of thought to the question after the ball, and had come to the conclusion he did not wish to spend his life without Abby. He decided that must be love. He had been intending to offer for her at once, but he would wait and see how the outing went, whether she regained her normal spirits, and whether there was sufficient time in between interruptions.

There were plenty of people driving and walking that afternoon, and he seemed to know most of them. They stopped almost every few yards to exchange greetings, and he was constantly introducing Abby to people who wondered who this new girl was. The young men invariably looked at her with approval, but he noted the occasional sour glance from girls he had in the past driven in his carriage, and even more speculative ones from mamas whose daughters had not been so honoured.

At one point he had to swerve sharply to avoid a curricle being driven erratically by two young men who seemed to be holding a rein each. The phaeton lurched to one side, and the earl threw his weight to the other side and managed to right it. He was, he realized, as he straightened up, practically lying on Abby.

'I do apologize,' he said. 'I hope I didn't hurt you?'

'I felt a trifle squashed,' she replied with more of her normal vivacity, 'but I understood the necessity. You reacted very promptly. We could have been lying on the ground now.'

'If I knew who those two confounded idiots were I'd take a whip to them!'

'If you did you'd mortally offend Lady Padmore. One of them was Caroline's brother Dudley. He has sold out of the army and arrived in Hill Street last week.'

'My own cousin, and I didn't recognize him?'

'I suspect he has changed. It must be some

time since you last saw him. Besides, you were too busy to take much notice of their features.'

'That's true. I think it's been four years since I saw him, just before he joined the army. He's of age now, so I don't have to supervise him. And the families were never close, it must be ten years or more since they visited us at Wantock House. I seem to recall trouble with him then, stealing a shotgun and trying to shoot Mama's pet poodle. Fortunately he had a rotten aim. I believe my father banished him then, and that is partly the reason we do not have a great deal to do with Lady Padmore.'

'She was pleased to see him, but I suppose any mother would be happy to see her son. He sold out because he did not wish to go to India. Very unenterprising!'

'Would you like to travel?'

'Of all things, but I would be content to return to Bath.'

The earl was silent. The near-accident, and Abby's unusual quietness, made him think it was not the best moment to declare himself. There would be plenty of other opportunities, when the circumstances would be more propitious.

8

Abby lay in wait for Dudley, and when he came into the house she emerged from the dining room.

'Dudley, may I have a few words?'

'Pretty one, of course you may. As many as you like.'

He was clearly intoxicated. Abby began to wonder if she had chosen the best time, but she wanted to confront him while her anger was still red hot. She glanced at the butler, and he slightly inclined his head, turning back towards the front door. Abby nodded to him and smiled. He would be within call. Lady Padmore's servants had quickly realized the sort of man Dudley was. Ellie, her own maid, had been indignant because he had tried to waylay the housemaid on the back stairs, and only the opportune arrival of Miss Browne had saved the girl from being roughly handled.

Abby retreated behind the table and Dudley, to her relief, collapsed into a chair.

'What is it?'

'You were driving a curricle this afternoon, in the Park.'

'Oh, you want me to take you for a drive, do you? In my new curricle. Though my dear mama doesn't yet know the bill will be sent to her. And your money will pay for it. So perhaps it's only fair I drive you out in it.'

'You are rambling! Did you realize you almost caused an accident with your idiotic driving? You almost upset Lord Wantock's phaeton. We could have been killed.'

'Oh dear, was that who it was? My precious cousin. That pretentious earl who looks down his aristocratic, long, twisted nose at me? What are you doing, driving with him? It's Caroline who's meant to marry him.'

Abby was almost diverted into refuting his description of the earl, but forced herself to keep to the point.

'You owe him and me an apology, and if I see you driving so wickedly in future, I'll — '

'You'll what, my pretty?'

Abby wondered just what threat would pierce his complacency.

'I'll tell your mother, and make sure she refuses to pay your debts!'

'Oh dear, I'm a naughty boy, am I? Need Nanny to spank me? But I'd prefer you to do that,' he said, suddenly rising from the chair and lunging across the table.

It was too wide for him to reach her and as, swearing, he began to move round it, Abby went the other way and escaped into the hall. How could Caroline have such an obnoxious brother?

* * *

Lady Quinton continued to host her dance breakfasts, though two of the young men had sent excuses.

'We need more men to make up the sets,' she complained. 'Caroline, dear, would your brother come?'

'I don't think so, my lady,' Caroline replied. 'He has never learned to dance, and said yesterday he never meant to do so.'

Abby was relieved. She did not know what she would have done if he had been included.

'I suppose he is rather young,' Lady Quinton said. 'Haven't any of you brothers or cousins you might ask to come?'

'If you don't consider them too old, I might be able to persuade a couple of my friends, former army officers, to join us,' the earl said. 'They know the steps, which would be an advantage.'

Lady Quinton looked a little dubious. Was she thinking the girls would be overawed? Privately Abby thought the girls and their mothers would be delighted to think they were mixing with older men rather than the somewhat callow youths who were almost the same ages as the debutantes.

The earl succeeded in drawing in two former soldiers, and as they were more experienced dancers Lady Quinton was able to allocate them to the different sets.

'Let's change partners,' Anne said, after the first session of instruction. 'There are now enough of us who know the steps, who can guide the others, and we can do the whole dance at once.'

This suggestion was applauded. A few of the girls, who tended to know more of the dances than the young men, had been murmuring about the disjointed nature of the dancing.

'We have to do the whole dance at Almack's,' one of them said. 'It will be good practice.'

The earl moved swiftly to Abby's side, and Hartley partnered Caroline. Anne, Abby was amused to see, was dancing with one of the earl's friends, and Lady Quinton was eyeing them with some disfavour.

Hartley stayed with Caroline for the rest of the morning, and escorted the girls back to Hill Street, even though Ellie, Abby's maid, had been sent with them as chaperon. Abby glanced from one to the other, seeing how absorbed they were in conversation, just as they had been at the breakfast, when they had sat aside from the others, talking all the time.

'Do you like Hartley?' she demanded, when they were safely inside the house, and Hartley, with some reluctance, had departed.

'He has more to talk about than some of the men we meet at Almack's,' Caroline replied. 'All some of them can talk about is gossip and fashion. I thought women were supposed to be guilty of that.'

Abby laughed. 'So what is so much more interesting?'

'Well, I never knew how many different things we imported from other countries. I'd never really considered it before. Muslin and silk and oranges and spices and so on were just in the shops. There has to be such a deal or organization to bring it here and then get it to customers.'

'Hartley knows all about that.'

'He does. And Abby, Cousin Julian has introduced him to Lady Cowper, and has permission to bring him to Almack's tomorrow! We'll be able to dance properly there. What shall I wear?'

★　★　★

They were sitting down to dinner that evening when there was the sound of an

144

arrival in the hall. Dudley, telling Caroline he had no desire to eat with a couple of dull spoil sports, was dining out, and for a moment Abby wondered if he had changed his mind, then as the butler opened the dining room door to announce the guest she heard Lady Jordan telling him not to disturb Lady Padmore.

Tossing down her napkin she rose to greet the newcomer.

'Aunt Emily! Oh, how wonderful to see you! But why did you not tell me you were coming?' she demanded, throwing her arms round Lady Jordan and hugging her tightly.

'My dear Abby. You look well, child. Hester, how good to see you. And this must be your daughter. But I did not mean to disturb your dinner.'

'Have you dined? Then do join us. When did you arrive? Where are you staying? I would offer you a room here, but since Dudley came home we have no spare guest rooms.'

'You need not be concerned. I wrote to an old friend that Abby was here, and she invited me to stay with her. She lives retired in Chelsea village, so you probably don't know her. A Mrs Mary Hughes. She was widowed many years ago, and has no children.'

'No, I don't know her, but you must come

and see us as often as she can spare you.'

Lady Jordan stayed until her hostess's carriage called for her two hours later, listening as Abby and Caroline told her about the parties and theatres they had been to.

'And I hear you obtained vouchers for Almack's. Is it still as dull as when I was a girl?'

'It won't be so dull once we are permitted to waltz,' Abby said. 'It is mortifying to have to sit out.'

'And watch the girls who have been given permission smirking at us,' Caroline added.

'My dear!' her mother protested. 'Even though you think that you must not show it. You will be given permission soon if you do nothing to offend the patronesses.'

Abby was thankful they had no engagements that evening, so she could go early to bed. Both Lady Padmore and Caroline were tired after a ceaseless round of engagements, and said they intended to retire early too, and take advantage of an early night.

As they went upstairs Caroline asked her why Dudley had been so rude to her.

'I'm used to him being rude to me,' she said, 'but he glared at you as though you had offended him.'

Abby had decided not to tell his mother or sister about Dudley's foolish behaviour in the

Park. By great good fortune, and the earl's swift action, there had been no accident, so she saw no purpose in worrying them. She made some light response, and the girls went into their own rooms.

Unable to sleep when she had retired to bed, Abby kept thinking about it, as she had done the previous night, shivering when she thought what might have happened, and shivering again when she recalled the earl's body pressed against hers.

Eventually she began to feel drowsy, and was almost asleep when a noise from downstairs brought her fully awake. She sat up in bed, wondering if they had burglars, then told herself not to be foolish. Burglars would not be carousing, singing very unmelodiously, if they were trying to rob a house.

She slipped out of bed, dragged on a robe, and went to the door. Her room and Caroline's were next door to one another, and Caroline was also at her bedroom door, clutching a shawl about her shoulders.

'What is it?' she demanded.

'I think it's your brother,' Abby replied, 'and it sounds as though he has a few friends with him.'

'It's three o'clock in the morning! How dare he make such a noise and wake us all up!'

'Hush, your mother is trying to talk to him.'

Lady Padmore's bedroom was on the floor below, and the two girls crept to the top of the flight and leaned over the banisters. They could see Dudley and at least two more young men in the hall on the ground floor. One of them was still singing in a loud tuneless voice, and clutching his companion round the neck.

'Dudley, do you realize what the time is?' his mother was asking. 'How dare you wake us all up like this!'

'You come in at this time when you've been to your precious parties,' Dudley said, and Abby thought he sounded just like a small boy. 'It's my house too, and if I want to bring my friends here for a game of cards I'll do it, whether you like it or not.'

'It is not your house. Your friends will leave at this moment, or I'll send for the Watch. They sound too drunk to play cards, anyway.'

'Besht go, ol' fellow,' one of the other men said. 'No shense in shtayin' if your old lady don't like us. Don't think she'll join us, shomehow.'

Caroline stifled a giggle. The girls saw Lady Padmore draw herself up and take a step towards the stairs. Down in the hall the butler and footman had appeared, partly dressed, and on the floor above Abby heard some of the maids whispering.

'Throw them out!' Lady Padmore ordered.

The butler, who was elderly, waited for the younger man to move first. The man who had not spoken became truculent, and tried to resist, but his friend grasped his arm and they staggered to the door which the butler had opened.

'Take no notice! You don't have to go! We were going to make a night of it, and you owe me revenge,' Dudley was protesting, trying to prevent his friends from leaving.

'Shut him out as well,' Lady Padmore said, and Dudley, hanging on to his friends in an attempt to prevent them from leaving, was dragged outside with them. The butler looked up to her ladyship, and on her gesturing to him to shut the door, did so.

'Throw the bolts. He can spend the night with one of them, the drunken sots.'

With which she turned and swept back into her bedroom, ignoring the hammering on the front door.

Abby and Caroline looked at one another.

'He'll keep us awake all night, Abby! And I'm so weary!'

'He'll soon grow tired of it; he's too drunk to make much effort. Do you know who the others were?'

'One of them was Harold Croft, I'm sure. I recognized his voice. Well, I don't think Mama will invite either him or his brother here again.'

They went back into their rooms, and Abby tried once more to get to sleep. Her room was on the front of the house, and she listened for a while to Dudley's hammering on the door, until someone in a house opposite leaned out of a window and threatened to shoot him unless he ceased his noise. After that the three young men, still singing raucously, went away, and she turned over and closed her eyes, but sleep still eluded her.

It was a pity Dudley could not be banished completely, Abby thought. He had not again attempted to kiss her, but every time they met he sneered at her, and if there was no one to hear he would make some disparaging comment about unknown chits who had to pay in order to be accepted into Society. She tried to ignore him, knowing he was trying to provoke her, but one day, she vowed, she would ignore him no longer. She just hadn't thought of a sufficiently horrible punishment yet, but she would, she knew, she soon would.

*   *   *

Abby and Caroline were beginning to feel quite at home at Almack's. They were by now acquainted with many people, and never lacked for partners. The only times they had to sit out were when waltzes were played.

Abby had been wondering where the earl was. It was almost eleven, the last waltz before supper was about to begin, and if he did not appear soon she would know he was not coming. It was difficult to hide her disappointment, but she had to turn a smiling face to Lady Padmore as that lady began to criticize the gowns worn by the debutantes who were dancing.

Then she gasped. The earl had just come into the ballroom. Hartley was with him, but she spared him just a swift glance. By now she knew the earl's features and figure well, often dreamed about him, but any sudden glimpse of him set her heart racing. He looked more handsome than ever. She hardly registered Lady Jersey walking between the two men until they stopped in front of her.

'Miss Barton, his lordship has asked me to give you permission to dance the waltz. And Miss Padmore, Mr Lennox wishes to dance with you. You both have my blessing.'

'Am I dreaming?' Abby asked, as the earl took her hand and led her on to the floor just as the music started.

He grinned at her and put his arm round her waist. She shivered, and could not think why, for she had danced the waltz with him at Lady Quinton's. He swung her into the dance, and she gave herself up to the rhythm, not speaking, her eyes half closed as they circled the floor.

'Don't go to sleep,' the earl said, laughter in his voice. 'Am I so very tedious a dancer?'

Abby's eyes snapped open.

'I'm not going to sleep! I'm just revelling in being able to waltz within these hallowed walls.'

He gave a choke of laughter.

'You, my dear girl, are an irreverent chit.'

'How did you persuade Lady Jersey to grant me her gracious permission to be held in a man's arms, in public?'

'Because she has no idea what a mockery you make of her and her friends.'

'Did you bring Hartley here?' Abby asked, suddenly recalling his unexpected appearance.

'I did. The poor fellow wants to experience all the pleasures London can offer.'

'Most of all he wants to be with Caroline. I've known Hartley all my life, and I've never known him pay so much attention to a girl before. Though I have to admit I don't know what he gets up to when he is in Bristol. He may have a dozen mistresses for all I know. He tells me most things, but I don't think a man would admit that sort of behaviour, do you?'

'Do — don't you mind if he pays Caroline attentions? He is your friend, after all.'

She chortled with laughter and almost missed a step. He tightened his arm about her and for a few moments they were closer than propriety allowed. Then, with a murmured apology he relaxed his grip.

'Are you asking me if I am jealous? If I wanted Hartley's attentions for myself? Of course I don't. I have no desire to marry him. It would be like marrying a brother. I think he and Caroline would deal together amazingly well, they like the same unexciting things. Oh dear, I shouldn't have said that. I do like both of them, truly, but — I think I had better not say any more.'

'Caroline likes him?'

'Yes, but her mother disapproves. Can you see her glaring at him now? I foresee you will be in trouble with her for introducing him here, especially so that they can waltz together. He is not the sort of husband she wants to snare for Caroline. A merchant, my dear! Impossible.'

He blinked. 'That sounded just like my cousin Padmore. Can you mimic others as well?'

'Yes, but Aunt Emily says it is a bad habit, and one day I will forget and mimic someone to their face. I can't mimic men, so you are quite safe.'

'How fortunate. That's the end of the dance. May I take you in to supper?'

* * *

Lady Padmore sat with pursed lips as they were driven back to Hill Street. She said nothing to Abby, but had caught sight of her in the supper room, sitting with Caroline and talking to her. From the fact that Caroline made no attempt to reply Abby deduced Lady Padmore was berating her. Hartley had disappeared after that one waltz, and Abby was a little disappointed in her friend if he had vanished from timidity, a reluctance to stand by Caroline to face her mother's disapproval.

Heavens, she thought crossly, one dance, even if it is a waltz, is scarcely a declaration. If Lady Padmore makes too much of this she will be more likely to put the idea of being in love with Hartley into Caroline's head than stop any budding attraction between them.

In silence they descended from the carriage. Abby glanced at the house and rather to her surprise saw that the curtains at the dining room windows were not completely drawn, and the glow from several candles shone through the gap.

The moment the front door opened she heard loud singing coming from the dining room.

Lady Padmore, after a slight pause, went across and flung open the door. Over her shoulder Abby could see half-a-dozen men sprawled round the table. Several decanters and wine bottles, some tipped over, one or two spilling wine, were scattered amongst broken wine glasses, and the men held cards in their hands. Piles of coins and slips of paper were in front of each player, and an untended cigar smouldered. It had already burned a hole in the surface of the table.

'Just what do you think you are doing?' Lady Padmore almost shrieked at them.

'Just a friendly party, ma'am,' one of the men, several years older than the rest, said, and smirked. 'Dudley is surely allowed to invite his friends into his home for a quiet game of cards?'

'Not drunken sots who ruin the furniture! All of you, the party is over. Leave the house before I send for the Watch.'

Dudley stood up, and had to cling to the back of the chair for support.

'If you inshult my friends, I'll have to — have to — what will I have to do?' he said, turning towards the older man.

'Find rooms where you can do as you like, not be under petticoat government at your age, my friend.'

'Thass right. My own rooms. Thass what I'll do. Come on. Let's go and find me shome rooms.'

Lady Padmore made no attempt to stop him as, helped by a pair of less intoxicated friends, he staggered past her and through the front door.

The butler looked on approvingly, and shot the bolts the moment the last of them were outside.

'I'll clear up what I can now, my lady.'

'Thank you. And don't let him back in.'

'Where will he sleep?' Caroline whispered to Abby, but Lady Padmore heard her.

'I have no notion. With his drunken friends, perhaps, or in the gutter. It makes no difference to me. Why am I plagued with such unsatisfactory children?'

9

Easter had passed, and it was the middle of April. Lady Quinton said there was no more point in having her dance breakfasts, since everyone now knew the steps. Abby suspected it was because the earl was unavailable. He had been forced to go to Wantock House, where his steward reported some problems with the roof, and wanted authorization to instigate repairs.

Abby missed him, and told herself not to be ridiculous. She now knew several young men, was never without a partner at Almack's or the other balls they attended, and had received two proposals, both of which she had refused. She was well aware the earl would never contemplate asking her to marry him, but she decided she could not contemplate marriage with anyone else. It followed she would remain a spinster, and every time they met she did her best to persuade Mr Wood that what she really wanted was her own business.

He told her to wait, saying the Season had barely started, and she had several more weeks to enjoy the balls, breakfasts, picnics, soirees, and theatre visits.

At least she had the pleasure of Aunt Emily's company, she told herself. In between their social engagements, Lady Padmore was busy compiling a list of people they must invite to her and Caroline's ball.

'You will stay for it, please,' Abby demanded of Lady Jordan. 'It's fixed for the middle of May, which is less than four weeks.'

'Of course I will, my dear. I want to see you in your ballgown.'

'And we must invite Mr Wood,' she told Lady Padmore.

'Oh, my dear, he is a City man. He would be out of place, uncomfortable with the *ton*.'

'I doubt Mr Wood would be uncomfortable anywhere,' Abby said, indignant. 'Besides, as my trustee he is paying for it, isn't he? It would be most insulting not to send an invitation. He can always make some excuse if he prefers not to come,' she added.

Not trusting Lady Padmore she made sure of sending the invitation herself, and was delighted when Mr Wood, once again driving her in his cabriolet, told her he would most certainly be attending.

'You have blossomed since you came to London, my dear. You look more and more like your dear mother. Have you chosen your ballgown yet?'

'Not yet, but we are going to Madame Cecile's soon to look at patterns.'

'You must not spare any expense on it, tell Lady Padmore.'

'I don't think she will skimp,' Abby said. 'She is eager to see me suitably settled, as well as Caroline, and she will not skimp on her gown, so she cannot on mine.'

'Am I to expect any suitors asking for your hand soon?'

Abby laughed. 'No, sir. There's no one here I want to marry.'

Which was strictly true, she consoled herself, for the earl was still out of London.

'Well, you cannot have met all the eligible young men yet. Perhaps I should let it be known that you can expect a substantial fortune.'

Abby shook her head.

'No, sir! Please do not. I have no wish to be courted for what a man expects to get in the way of money.'

He smiled reminiscently.

'All for love, eh? Like your mother.'

* ★ *

The earl returned a week later, and when he met Abby at Almack's he suggested making up a party to ride out to Richmond Park.

'The weather is warm for April. I thought Caroline and Anne might come, and any other girls you would like to invite. Your friend Mr Lennox would come, I'm sure, and my old friend Thomas Swanson is very taken with Anne.'

In the end a party of a dozen people set off a few days later. The earl had a new mount, a sleek chestnut gelding, and Abby looked admiringly at him when they met. She watched the horse curvetting playfully, but obeying his rider's commands instantly. She longed to ride him. In Bath, and here in London, she was provided with safe, unexciting hacks, but she knew she was a competent rider, and was sure the chestnut was well mannered enough to tolerate her.

They fell naturally into pairs as they rode westwards. The earl led the way with Abby, but Caroline and Hartley lingered until they were at the rear. Anne was with Thomas Swanson, one of the men the earl had introduced to the dance breakfasts. He was being very attentive to Anne, dancing with her whenever they were at the same ball, and she had confided to Abby and Caroline that she expected him to make her an offer. She had, she told them rather shamefacedly, decided she did not after all wish to marry their neighbour, John Webster.

'Though Mama does not favour Thomas,' she sighed, 'because he does not have a title. His family is as old as ours, though, and he has a fine estate in Yorkshire and a good income.'

Titles seemed to be what parents and guardians looked for, Abby thought. No doubt Thomas's parents would welcome Anne, from a titled family, even if hers were dubious in return, because Thomas was not. The earl's mother and sister would be yet more dubious, scandalized even, if he ever suggested marrying her, a nobody.

She did her best to throw off gloomy reflections, and admire the countryside. The trees were showing fresh new green, spring flowers covered the fields, and lambs were gambolling round their mothers. At Richmond they admired the herds of deer, and then repaired to an inn where a nuncheon had been ordered.

After eating they strolled in the Park until it was time to set off again. Abby glanced at Caroline, who was pink-cheeked and smiling. She and Hartley had wandered away from the rest, never out of sight, but out of hearing. In Bath she had occasionally teased him when he had shown an interest in any of the girls they met there, but they had all been light, frivolous flirtations. He was paying more serious attentions to Caroline, and she hoped neither of her friends would be hurt when it was time for him to return to Bath.

* * *

Mr Wood was spending an evening at the East and West club, which was a few doors away from his own house in St James's Square. He ordered dinner, and tried a new dish, veal served with a mushroom and cream sauce, and an ingredient he could not identify.

'Give the chef my compliments,' he told the waiter when a bottle of claret was placed on the table afterwards.

'Of course, sir. Are you going into the rooms tonight?'

'Not to play. I'll look in later.'

An hour later, after he had shared another bottle of claret with an old friend, he went upstairs to the card rooms. The faro tables were busy, he noted, but he did not join them. Other games, cards and backgammon, were being played at small tables. He went on to where a hazard table had attracted a rather noisy group of young men. One, he noted, raising his eyebrows, was young Hartley Lennox, Abby's friend from Bath. Another, and he frowned, for there had been trouble with him a few nights before when he had been forced to intervene, was Dudley Padmore.

He stayed to watch for a while, but the dealer seemed to be in control, so he moved on. He was going past the table when his name was called.

'Mr Wood! A word, if you please.'

It was young Padmore, and he sounded tipsy. Mr Wood turned to walk back towards him.

'Yes? Can I help you?'

Dudley sniggered. 'You can settle a dispute here. No one knows how much the Barton filly is worth, if she's worth the bother of making up to. I say at least ten thousand a year. You're her trustee, you must know.'

Mr Wood clenched his hands into fists, and with difficulty refrained from punching the young jackanapes in the teeth. He looked down his nose at the group, and noticed Hartley looking distressed. He was a different sort from Padmore, and because Abby liked him Mr Wood hoped he was not getting into bad company.

'That, young man, is between me and any honest man who offers for her. It's not public information for scoundrels like you to drool over.'

Padmore started towards him, but was pulled back by Hartley and one of his friends.

After a short struggle he permitted them to thrust him back into his chair, and Mr Wood went on.

As he left the club, he had a few words with the doorman, and a few minutes later, watching from the window of his study, had the satisfaction of seeing Dudley Padmore and his companions emerge from the club, loudly arguing where they might go next. Hartley Lennox, he was pleased to see, walked swiftly away from them. He hoped the boy had learned his lesson, and would in future avoid such unsavoury company.

* * *

All the way to the Park Caroline had been smiling to herself, but refused to explain the reason to Abby.

'Wait until we're alone,' she whispered, glancing about her.

Since the only other people around at this early hour were a few men on horseback, delivery boys, and maids sweeping the steps or polishing the knockers on the front doors, Abby felt her caution was superfluous, but she waited in patience. Caroline would not for long be able to resist telling her whatever it was.

She was proved right. They had no sooner

passed through the gate and moved away from the few riders than Caroline seized her hand and squeezed it.

'At the ball last night,' she began, 'did you notice anything special?'

Abby shook her head, amused.

'What sort of special? That quiz of a dowager wearing the purple turban? Or Harold Croft with his cravat that was coming undone, and he never noticed it?'

Caroline laughed. 'Of course not. Hartley. Did you see him?'

'Well, yes, I usually see him at the balls and other entertainments we attend. I sometimes wonder who tells him where we are going to be,' she added innocently.

'You know very well he asks me or you!'

Abby looked at Caroline's flushed cheeks and decided to be merciful.

'He was looking exceptionally pleased with himself, I thought, but I assumed it was because he had mastered tying the Mathematical at last. He's been struggling with it for years.'

'Abby! Don't joke! He asked me to marry him,' she said in a rush.

Abby considered the joyful expression on Caroline's face. Or besotted, she corrected her thoughts, and sighed inwardly. She had seen how absorbed they were with one another, but could foresee nothing but problems. Hartley was not the husband Lady Padmore would want for Caroline.

'Does your mother know?'

'Of course not, and we are not going to tell her for a while. Hartley means to go home and ask his uncles what they will do for him. He says he has an adequate allowance now, ample for us to live on, but they promised him more when he married, and he gets something when he is five and twenty. He wants to be able to tell Mama his fortune is respectable.'

'Your mother wanted you to marry your cousin, and if she could not contrive that, someone with a title,' Abby said carefully.

Privately she thought Lady Padmore would never give Caroline permission to marry someone from merchant stock, unless he had an enormous fortune. Hartley and his mother lived modestly in Bath. They gave no indication of possessing more than a competence, and she had no idea how prosperous the business in Bristol was.

Had she any right to interfere, even to warn Caroline that she might encounter opposition? She looked at Caroline's happy expression and decided she could not bear to cast any doubts and dim that joyous expectation.

'I'm not at all interested in titles,' Caroline said. 'After all, it's my life, I will be the one with or without a title, and if I don't care, why should anyone else?'

'Parents will always want the best for their children, and to many of the *ton*, it seems to me, titles are even more important than a fortune.'

'Are you not happy for me?'

Abby thrust aside her doubts and hugged Caroline.

'I am delighted if you have found the man you love and want to spend the rest of your life with.'

'I shall be faithful to him, whatever people say,' Caroline said, showing for the first time a glimmer of doubt.

'Of course you will. It wouldn't be love if you were not.'

'I don't suppose they will beat me, or lock me up and feed me on bread and water,' she said, but her voice trembled slightly.

'You have only to stay firm. I suspect, if you either do not attract any better offers, or refuse any you do receive, by the end of the Season your mama will be glad to accept Hartley. After all, she will not be able to give you another Season, will she?'

'Not in Hill Street. And not without your money.'

'So don't encourage anyone else. If you find anyone paying you unusual attentions, tell me or Anne, and we will do our best to deter them.'

'How?' Caroline giggled. 'I know you are both prettier and more lively than I am, so will you try to persuade them to pay attentions to you instead?'

'I don't think Anne would agree to do that for fear it offended Thomas. Don't be concerned, I'll think of something.'

As they walked home she refused to tell Caroline what she might do, but her mind was whirling with schemes from whispering to these importunate suitors that there was insanity in the Padmore family, or that Lady Padmore was grossly in debt. She doubted whether Caroline was strong enough to withstand her mother's arguments, and Lady Padmore would be furious when she discovered the truth.

★ ★ ★

The earl was back in town, and went to Lady Padmore's box at the opera during the first interval. His own box was opposite, and he had watched in mingled amusement and irritation how Gregory Croft behaved. He paid no attention to the stage, but talked loudly throughout the performance, took snuff and sneezed loudly, and seemed to be urging Abby to join him in pointing out people they knew in the other boxes.

Abby, he could see, was annoyed, and kept trying to hush him, or when he tried to engage her in conversation, pointedly ignored him and concentrated on what was happening on stage.

Apart from Mrs Croft, there was a lady he did not know in the party, but she and Abby seemed fond of one another, and well acquainted, judging by the delighted glances that passed between them when one of the singers performed particularly well.

He discovered, when they were introduced, that she was Lady Jordan, who had been Abby's substitute mother in Bath. She seemed a sensible woman, he decided. She must be if she had brought up Abby.

During his time in the country his determination to have Abby as his wife had increased. He would have asked her weeks ago, if estate business had not intervened, but he meant to lose no time in proposing. He managed to draw her into a corner at the back of the box just before the interval ended.

'Will you drive with me tomorrow?'

'Will you let me take the reins? Just for a short, short while,' she wheedled, and Julian, who had never thought he would ever permit a female to drive any of his cattle, found himself contemplating doing just that. She was a witch.

'We'll see,' he said, and then had to leave as the second act was about to begin.

He could barely control his impatience the following day, and arrived in Hill Street promptly at four. As he drew to a halt outside Lady Padmore's house Dudley emerged, slamming the door after him, and stalked towards Berkeley Square. Tossing the reins to his tiger he went to the front door, expecting Abby to be waiting for him. Unlike other damsels he had in the past favoured with his attentions, she was refreshingly straightforward. Not for her were the tricks designed to make him more eager, such as keeping him waiting, debating for five minutes altogether whether the chosen hat was suitable for an open carriage, in a blatant attempt to elicit compliments, or asking whether it was warm enough for the pelisse or ought she to take a cloak.

Rather to his surprise his knock on the door went unanswered for several minutes. Then the butler opened it and mutely gestured him to enter.

Once inside he could hear hysterical shrieks coming from the drawing room on the next floor. He looked at the butler, who shrugged.

'Is someone ill?'

'Her ladyship, my lord. She has suffered a severe shock. Miss Barton asked me to say she very much regrets that she cannot drive with you, she feels it necessary to stay with her ladyship.'

'She is well?'

The butler leaned close and sank his voice to a whisper.

'Oh, yes, my lord. If I may say so, Miss Barton is the only one keeping her head, and I do not know how we would be going on if she were not here to manage things.'

'Can I help?'

'I don't think so, my lord. The doctor has been sent for.'

'Then will you please tell Miss Barton that I will call for her tomorrow, at the same time, and hope she will be free to drive with me then.'

★　★　★

Abby was changing ready for the drive, attaching her new chip straw hat, when she heard Dudley's voice, raised to a shout, from the landing below. Caroline was weeping noisily, and Lady Padmore berating them both.

She slipped out on to the landing and leaned over the banisters. Caroline was crouched on the stairs, her head in her hands, while Dudley raved at her, jabbing his fingers at her.

'I saw them! I came back to pick up my things, and they didn't know I was here. They thought they were private, sneaking into the dining room! How can you permit it?'

'I don't permit it!' Lady Padmore shrieked, her voice shrill with emotion. 'How can I keep my eyes on her every hour of the day? It isn't as though you are here to help.'

'You turned me out, if you remember. But you can't permit my sister to disgrace us all by kissing a low-down fellow nobody knows, who reeks of the shop, and doesn't have any of the proper instincts of a gentleman. He was kissing her, my sister!'

Caroline looked up, and brushed the tears from her eyes.

'I'm betrothed to Hartley! I'm going to marry him! And he has more gentlemanly instincts than you do!'

'You are not marrying that fellow. You are here, spending money I could do with, trying to get a respectable alliance. Even if you can't snare our blessed cousin Julian and his title, you'll not disgrace us all by being taken in by a shop-crawling nobody!'

'I don't want to marry Cousin Julian! I never have done. And it's Abby's money, not yours!'

'Yes, and no doubt she introduced you to the damned fellow. He's a friend of hers, isn't he? Two low-down frauds who've wangled their way into the family!'

Abby decided she had heard enough. She descended the stairs.

'Have you finished abusing me and my friend Hartley?' she asked, her voice dripping with scorn. 'Let me tell you Mr Lennox is worth a dozen of you. He does not indulge in drunken orgies in his mother's house, or harangue his mother in the way you are doing. A fine exhibition you are making of yourself in front of the servants. No doubt all of Hill Street and beyond will know just what sort of scum you are before tomorrow.'

He stepped towards her and grasped at her shoulder, trying to twist her round, but she had armed herself with a long, sharp hatpin, and without any compunction she dug it into his hand. As he gasped and looked at the puncture in astonishment, then began to suck the drops of blood, she turned to Lady Padmore and urged her into the drawing room.

'Lie down, ma'am, and I will send for Miss Browne. You need a restorative to calm your nerves. Caroline, help me with your mother. Dudley, I suggest you take your leave.'

After settling a wildly weeping Lady Padmore on a sopha she drew the still moist Caroline to one side.

'Where is Hartley?'

Caroline had difficulty in suppressing her frightened tears sufficiently to answer, then her words poured out in a torrent. Abby had to concentrate to make sense of the muffled explanation.

'I told him to go. He came to say farewell; he's off to Bath tomorrow. Dudley was trying to fight him, call him out. I couldn't bear it if they had a duel. Dudley is a good swordsman, and a good shot, they taught him in the army, but Hartley has never used either of them!'

'Nevertheless he should have stayed to support you,' Abby said, disappointed in her old friend. 'He should have knocked Dudley down.'

'He wanted to, but I wouldn't let him. When Mama is like this she won't listen to anyone. It's hopeless. I told him to come back tomorrow, and not go to Bath until the following day. Then we can all talk it over quietly.'

Abby doubted it.

'I must go and send a message to Lord

Wantock. I cannot leave you to drive with him this afternoon.'

She gave the message to the butler, who was hovering outside the drawing room, and asked him to send for Lady Padmore's doctor. When she returned, it was to find Lady Padmore still in hysterics, pushing away the smelling salts Caroline was holding out to her, moaning about the ingratitude of her children, and wishing she was in her grave, where they no doubt were trying to send her.

Abby sighed and went across to take the smelling salts from the still lachrymose Caroline.

'Go and lie down,' she advised quietly. 'Dudley is gone, and when you are no longer here I'm sure she will be calmer.'

'You mean the sight of me upsets her,' Caroline sniffed.

'Yes,' Abby said, though it was her opinion that when there was no one present to listen to her complaints, Lady Padmore's hysterics would quickly subside.

She greeted Miss Browne's entrance with relief, handed over the smelling salts, said she was going to see that Caroline was all right, and thankfully escaped.

10

Lady Padmore remained prostrated, refusing to see anyone apart from Miss Browne and her doctor. Hartley came to Hill Street early on the following day, and because Lady Padmore had not thought to tell the butler to deny him, he, Caroline and Abby met in the drawing room to consider tactics.

Caroline was pale and her eyes were red from continuous weeping. She sat on a sopha beside Hartley and clung to his hand as he and Abby discussed what best to do.

'You will do no good remaining in Town,' Abby told him.

'I don't want him to go!' Caroline wailed. 'I need him here, to support me against Dudley and Mama.'

'Anne and I will support you, but don't you see, if Hartley can obtain promises of a good income from his uncles, your mama might be persuaded to accept him. Especially if you remain firm and refuse any other offers.'

'I haven't had any other offers,' Caroline said.

Abby detected a note of petulance in her voice. Was she jealous of the two offers Abby had received, even though both had been rejected? At the time she had laughed with Abby, and applauded her for rejecting them, but then she had been in expectation of Hartley's making a declaration. And however much she and Anne teased Abby about Lord Wantock's attentions, Abby was sure neither of them really expected him to offer for her. She did not herself.

'Go home, talk to your mama, and your uncles,' Abby insisted. 'When you come back, don't call here. We can meet in the Park when I take Rusty for walks. Then come to our ball. It's less than two weeks away.'

'Why shouldn't he call here?' Caroline asked.

'We don't want to give your mother an excuse for banning him from your ball. If she doesn't see him she will most likely forget he had an invitation. She won't be able to make a fuss there and, as it's my ball too, and Hartley is a friend of mine, he will be there at my personal invitation.'

'She'll be furious with you.'

'What can she do? She will scarcely send me back to Bath, or she would have to give up the house, and all hope of establishing you respectably.'

'Hartley is respectable!'

'I didn't say he was wasn't. Don't fire up at

me, I'm trying to help you both.'

Abby was beginning to feel impatient with Caroline. She could think only of the misery she would suffer if she were not able to see Hartley at every ball or breakfast or ridotto she went to, and nothing about how to deal with her mother for the longer term.

'I'm sorry.' Caroline began to weep again, and Hartley gathered her to him and patted her shoulder.

'Don't be so hard on her, Abby. She's not as tough as you. But I will set off today. I can reach Bristol tomorrow, and be back in Town two days later, at most. What you say makes sense, and we'll meet in the Park whenever we can, in the mornings. I'll stay out of sight the rest of the day, so that no one sees me and tells Lady Padmore.'

'Or Dudley!'

Caroline sounded frightened.

'I'm not afraid of him.'

'He'll tell his mother,' Abby warned.

'He'll try to force you into a duel!'

'He won't succeed. If he killed me he'd have to go abroad. Caroline, my dear, I ought to go if I'm to reach Marlborough, or perhaps Calne, if I am lucky, tonight.'

Abby escorted him to the front door, making sure none of the servants saw him. She would speak to the butler later, but she

178

was sure he disliked Dudley, and was sympathetic to Caroline, and would therefore not consider it his duty to inform Lady Padmore of Hartley's visit.

'Look after her,' Hartley said as they parted. 'She doesn't have your strength.'

She could do with a little more firmness, Abby thought, and after he had gone she took herself back to the drawing room with the intention of trying to stiffen Caroline's spine.

* * *

Because of Lady Padmore's continuing indisposition, she was unable to escort the girls to the various engagements they had made for the following week. Lady Padmore would not see Caroline, and even refused to see Dudley when he called, which he did regularly every day. Abby did not even try to see her.

Hartley returned, and they met twice in the Park that week. He had secured promises from his uncles of a large increase in his allowance, and they proposed buying him a house in Clifton as a wedding present. As he described it to them, Caroline exclaimed that it would be larger and more imposing than their own house in Devon, which was just a small manor house with only the home farm

179

and a few acres of parkland left. Her father had been forced to sell all the unentailed property to fund his extravagant lifestyle and increasing gambling debts.

Lady Jordan, calling one day, heard all about it from Abby.

'Can some other lady not escort you to your parties? It seems a great shame you have to forego them, the Season is so short.'

'Caroline would not go, and people might think us unfeeling.'

'Perhaps big parties would be wrong, but surely you could attend the theatre, or small, select gatherings of friends? If I can be of any help I will chaperon you both. I will go and speak to Lady Padmore and suggest it.'

'She is refusing to see anyone,' Abby warned.

'Then I will write her a note.'

She sat down at the escritoire and did so immediately, and it was sent to Lady Padmore's room. The effect was, Abby considered, little short of miraculous. Lady Jordan was summoned to the sickroom, and returned to the drawing room half an hour later, bringing Caroline, who had been in her own room, with her.

'Caroline's mama is feeling so much restored after her rest, she proposes to get up for dinner, and perhaps, if the weather is clement, take a short drive tomorrow. I believe you planned to go to the theatre tomorrow evening? She hopes she will be well enough to take you. Caroline, she wishes to see you now.'

Caroline cast a haunted glance at Abby, but obediently left the room.

'Did she mention Hartley?'

'No. She blamed her indisposition on too much exertion, too many parties. Is Hartley back in Town?'

'Yes, but he is staying away from all the parties so that he does not remind Lady Padmore of his existence.'

'I fear that will be in vain. When I knew Hester as a girl she was one of the most determined, I might almost say stubborn, people I had ever met. I doubt she has changed. If Caroline truly loves Hartley she will have to show the same stubbornness.'

* * *

The earl, meeting Hartley as he rode in the Park one morning, stopped and asked him if he knew how Lady Padmore did.

'I understand she is ill,' he said, 'as neither she nor the girls have been seen for several days. When I asked Abby to drive with me she sent a message saying she could not leave

Caroline. Is she ill too?'

'She is in low spirits,' Hartley told him. 'I have just left her. It is the only time we may meet in safety. Are you aware I offered for Caroline, and that is what has caused her mother to stage this collapse?'

'Oh dear, you think it is not genuine?'

'I am sure it is not. She hates the notion of Caroline marrying a merchant, and hopes by this means to detach her from me.'

'Will she succeed?' Julian asked bluntly.

Hartley passed a hand over his brow.

'I really don't know. When I see Caroline she swears she will be firm, and has not changed in her affection for me, but she is not so strong willed as her mother. And Dudley is there every day, haranguing her, and trying to poison her mind against me. He tried to challenge me to a duel before I went to Bristol.'

'Perhaps I had better have a word with him.'

'I don't need you to fight my battles, my lord.'

'Don't be a gudgeon. They are my cousins. I mean to tell him that if he annoys Caroline he will have me to answer to as well as you. I'm fond of the chit, she's the best of her family.'

'They go to the theatre tonight, but I

cannot be seen there. Perhaps you might go and see for yourself how Caroline is?'

Julian promised to do that. He wanted to see Abby, and if possible have a private word with her. If Lady Padmore were once more able to go about, he had an opportunity to see Abby and make his offer.

*   *   *

Anne had joined them in the Park that morning, and they accompanied her back to Berkeley Square for breakfast. Lady Quinton soon left them, saying she had a fitting at the modiste's, so they were able to talk freely about Caroline's situation.

'You must not give in,' Anne insisted. 'They'll have to permit you to marry eventually.'

'Eventually? But I won't be twenty-one for almost three years. That's an age to wait.'

'You could elope to Gretna Green,' Anne suggested. 'That would be exciting, riding through the night, dreading pursuit, but knowing that at the end of it you and your beloved Hartley would be together.'

'And disowned by her mother and brother?' Abby asked. 'My mother eloped, and I don't even know who my grandparents were. They apparently vowed never to speak to her again.'

'I'd forgotten. I'm sorry. But she must have thought being with your father more important than obeying her parents. They were unreasonable, like Caroline's mama. She died when you were a baby, didn't she? Perhaps if she had not they would have forgiven her in time.'

'And perhaps not. They did not offer to take me in. My father must have left money — my trustee has been able to pay for Lady Jordan to bring me up, and for my come out, and he says there is money for me when I marry.'

'Who was your father? There are several families called Barton, but Mama does not know of any where a son eloped with an heiress.'

'So you all talk of me, do you? And as far as I know my mama had no money. Her parents would not have given her any. It's likely that she was cut off from money as well as family.'

Anne nodded. 'She might have inherited from a godmother or someone else. I really don't understand how these trusts and things work. But that doesn't help Caroline. Is there any money coming to you when you are of age?'

Caroline shook her head. 'Our family has no money, apart from a small amount which Papa couldn't touch, Mama's jointure, and the rents of one farm and a couple of cottages at home. We have to live on that, and of course, what Mr Wood paid Mama for bringing out Abby.'

'So if you elope you are not going to lose any money,' Anne said. 'Your mama might even be grateful as she need not support you any longer. Besides, you must be practical, and without any fortune you are unlikely to attract many offers. Merchants can be wealthy. She may realize that in the end and be reconciled.'

The notion did not appear to appeal to Caroline. She insisted she would be too terrified to elope, for fear they were captured and Hartley thrown into prison on a charge of abduction.

'He might even be transported! I could not bear to lose him like that.'

'Can you bear to lose him any other way? Caroline, you have to be firm, and strong, and just refuse to marry anyone else, and it will all come right in the end.'

Caroline could not be comforted, and as she and Abby walked back to Hill Street she complained that Anne was too much influenced by the gothic romances she was so fond of reading.

'But I don't know what to do! I hate being scolded all the time, and sometimes I want so much to have it all as it was. I'm afraid I might give way.'

'You won't,' Abby tried to reassure her. 'You have me as well as Anne and Hartley to support you. Why don't you appeal to your cousin? Perhaps if he spoke to your mama she might relent.'

'She still thinks she will be able to persuade him to make me an offer, and Abby, if he did, they would force me to accept!'

'No one can force you to the altar, you goose! And I'm sure your cousin would have nothing to do with an unwilling bride.'

*   *   *

Despite Caroline's apparent acceptance of Abby's reassurances, when the earl appeared in their box at the theatre that night she shrank back in her chair with a squeak of alarm. He looked at her in some surprise and, after he had greeted Lady Padmore and Mrs Croft, nodded to the Croft brothers, and smiled at Abby, he sat beside her and asked how she did.

'You look pale,' he said bluntly. 'Have you been ill as well?'

'No, no, of course not.'

'Then come and walk with me for a while, where we can talk privately.'

She shrank even further back and shook her head, but he laughed and took her hand in his, forcing her to rise and accompany him out of the box. Lady Padmore looked on approvingly, and with an air of benevolence, suggested to Harold Croft that he and Abby might take a turn as well.

'Suitable for a younger son, with what I believe is a modest fortune,' Abby heard her say as she took Harold's arm and permitted him to lead her from the box.

'Miss Barton, how pleasant to be alone with you,' Harold said as they began to promenade in the area behind the boxes.

Abby glanced at the fashionable crowd around them.

'Hardly alone, sir. It's difficult to move above a very slow pace.'

'Alone in the midst of a crowd,' he declaimed, and she giggled. 'I am so looking forward to your ball next week. Pray, you will give me the pleasure of your hand for the first waltz, will you not?'

Abby frowned. She had been wondering for some time whether the earl would show any preference for her by soliciting her hand for a waltz, and did not wish to miss the opportunity by engaging herself too early to anyone else, particularly not to someone she did not like, and she had decided long ago she did not like the Croft brothers, cronies as they were of Dudley.

'I value your request,' she said untruthfully, 'but I do not intend to fill my card until the night itself. As it is my ball, as well as Caroline's, I believe it is my duty to hold myself free for dancing with important guests.'

'So I'm not important enough, am I?'

His tone was jocular, but beneath it she could detect a controlled anger. Did the man really believe in his charms so much that he thought she might be amenable to a match with him? She looked at him candidly and decided she really did not care if she offended him. She removed her hand from where it had rested on his arm and turned back towards the box.

'You are a younger son, you have no title and, as far as I know, no fortune. The sole purpose of my being in London, I am told, is to snare a rich, and if possible titled, husband. You must see therefore I cannot damage my opportunities by spending time with you when I might be enticing a more eligible husband.'

'More eligible! If you think I would ever offer for a nameless hussy like you, Miss Barton, whatever your fortune, you are very much mistaken. To even suggest it is an impertinence. We are an old, respected family.'

'Then it is a great pity you don't remember it when you are in your cups. Let us go back now,' she added, and within a minute was back in the box. Harold did not follow her, and when his mother asked where he was she said airily that she had no notion.

She had not seen the earl and Caroline, and assumed he had led her to a more secluded spot so that they could talk without interruption. For a brief moment she wondered whether he had succumbed to the pressure from Lady Padmore and meant to offer for Caroline, but a further moment's reflection showed her the unlikelihood of this. He showed no preference for her, had never taken her up in his carriage, and only ever danced country dances with her.

Caroline returned to the box just as the second act began and, as her seat was behind and at the other side of the box to Lady Padmore's, her mama could not demand to know what they had been talking about. Caroline looked calm, and when Abby raised her eyebrows she smiled back, reaching across and squeezing her hand.

Abby had to contain herself in patience while they watched the rest of the play, but to her relief Lady Padmore declared she did not wish to stay for the farce, so they were driven home before midnight.

In the coach Lady Padmore tried to discover what the earl had said, but Caroline told her he just wanted to talk about arrangements for the ball.

'Why should he consult you? The countess and I are making all the arrangements. In fact, I am going to see her tomorrow to discuss some final arrangements. What did he want to ask you?'

'Oh, what sort of dances I wanted, the sort of music, that is all,' Caroline said.

'How very odd. But perhaps it is a good sign that he is taking an interest in what will please you. You see, my dear, there are far better men than that impertinent fellow from Bath who could become attached to you. Abigail, what did young Harold have to say? He would be an excellent match for you, and he is interested, from what his mama told me.'

'I told him I could not be spending time with him when I might be enticing a more eligible husband,' Abby said.

'What? Abigail, tell me you are joking me! How could you be so lacking in caution as to offend someone who was showing interest in you!'

'Interest in whatever fortune I might have,

ma'am. I have no wish to encourage either of the Croft brothers to offer for me.'

'You need not imagine the older one will offer! Elder sons know their value. The best you can hope for, with your dubious inheritance, and unknown background, is a younger son.'

'If my background is unknown, how can my inheritance be called dubious?'

'You are impertinent!'

'So was he.'

No more was said. Lady Padmore maintained an offended silence, bade Abby a cold goodnight and went straight to her bedroom. Caroline seized Abby's hand and pulled her up the next flight of stairs.

'Abby,' she whispered, when they reached the sanctuary of her room, 'Cousin Julian said he would help me, support me if I really wanted Hartley. I told him Hartley was coming to our ball, and he said that afterwards he would speak to Mama.'

'Then, if you are firm too, I think your troubles will soon be over. I hope so.'

* * *

Mr Wood was startled the following day when his butler informed him that a lady wished to speak to him. He had remained in St James's

191

Square that morning to write letters and catch up with business unconnected to his dealings in the City, and was in his dressing room changing ready to go to his office.

'Who is it?' he asked, wondering whether Abby was asking for him.

The butler proffered a card, and he read the name with astonishment. What did Julian Wantock's sister want with him?

'Show her into my library, tell her I will join her in a few minutes, and bring some ratafia, please.'

He went downstairs shortly, and found an elderly maid sitting on a chair in the entrance hall. She glared at him before dropping her gaze, and he wondered why she looked so inimical. What had he ever done to offend her or her mistress?

'Lady Jane,' he said, walking across the room to where the earl's sister was standing in front of the window, looking out into the square. 'To what do I owe this pleasure?'

She turned slowly and surveyed him from head to toe, and her lip curled. He was irresistibly reminded of an extremely bad actress he had once seen perform in a melodrama, demonstrating contempt and scorn. He stifled the urge to laugh.

'It is no pleasure to me, sir. I have only yesterday learned, thanks to my cousin Sir

Dudley Padmore, that you are the owner of a disreputable gaming hell. I find it deplorable that you have thrust a girl connected to such on to my family, and I insist you remove her at once, before the whole *ton* discovers the shame of it.'

'Won't you sit down and let us discuss this reasonably?'

'I will not sit with a card sharper! I merely want your assurance that your ward — if she is indeed your ward — will not be present at the ball to be held at my family home next week.'

'I thought your family home, your London house, at least, was in Clarges Street? The ball you refer to is being held at your brother's house.'

She snorted, and began to pace up and down the room. He poured a glass of ratafia and held it out to her, but she waved it aside and he only just managed to keep it from spilling. He poured Madeira for himself, and sipped it, watching her perambulations with a detached air which seemed to stoke her anger.

'Whatever. It is an insult to him and my mother to introduce such a girl to them, let alone trick them into sponsoring her come out!'

'My lady, let me disabuse you of some of

your ideas. Yes, I do own the East and West, but it is a perfectly respectable club, as are White's and Brooks's. I am not, and never have been, a card sharper, and I advise you to withdraw that slander. If I find you repeating it I will take steps to silence you, through the courts if necessary.'

'How dare you threaten me!'

'No threats, that is a promise, my lady. As for Miss Barton, she is not my ward. I am the trustee of her fortune, and I can assure you that her parents were as well born as you.'

'Then why does she not know who they are? As she has admitted.'

'I think you are aware her mother was disowned by her family when she married against their wishes. When she was dying she begged that her daughter should not be told who they were.'

'All this is a mere quibble, and cannot be proven.'

'I do not have any obligation to prove anything to you. As for the ball, that is a matter between your mother and Lady Padmore.'

'They can hold the ball for my cousin, but I will protest if you try to insinuate your ward, or whatever she is, into the house clinging to Caroline's skirts.'

'I cannot believe you are unaware of the

fact that my money, or rather Abby's money, is paying for all this? If anyone is clinging to skirts it is Caroline and her mother clinging to Abby's.'

'If her father was a crony of yours, her money was no doubt won, by unfair means, from men who ruin themselves gambling in clubs like yours!'

'Actually most of my income arises from my dealings in the City.'

'What does that matter? It is another form of gambling. Will you prevent that girl from coming to my mother's house?'

'No, my lady, I will not.'

'Very well. I can threaten too. I shall go at once to my mother and demand she rescinds her invitation to that girl. If she sets foot across the threshold everyone in Town will know what she is.'

'If you try to prevent her from attending her own ball, my lady, none of the bills, and I understand there have been many already, will be paid. I am financing the ball for both Abby and your cousin. If I withdraw my support I think there would be a greater scandal than any you think you can devise.'

She stood looking at him, breathing deeply.

'You are not a gentleman!'

He almost laughed.

'Come, let us discuss this calmly.'

'I am calm! You will regret this!'

He was not in time to open the door for her as, trying to look as though she had triumphed, she swept out of the room. He sat down to finish his Madeira, poured another glass, and wondered whether she would attempt to ruin the ball for Abby. Ought he to speak to Lord Wantock, to warn him? But that would appear to be interference in his family, and he did not wish to cause trouble if Lady Jane's threats should turn out to be hot air.

Besides, he had often seen the earl and Abby together when they had not been aware of his scrutiny, and he had a fair notion of the feelings of both. If Lord Wantock decided that his position prevented him from offering for Abby he suspected she would be devastated. Any hint of a disagreement with his sister might just tip the balance and prevent such a declaration. He would do nothing, but keep a close watch on things.

11

Abby considered she exercised a remarkable degree of self-control not to intervene when Lady Padmore and Dudley continued to demand from Caroline a promise she give up all notions of marrying Hartley. Dudley, with a considerable lack of grace, had given up his independent set of rooms and moved back to Hill Street. Abby suspected he had run out of funds and needed free lodgings.

At first she had protested at their bullying, but Caroline had begged her not to, and when she saw how distressed the arguments made her friend she kept her mouth shut. She could not control the looks of disgust and anger, though, and found she was being chastised for them almost as much as Caroline was for her stubbornness.

Finally Caroline could withstand the pressure no more. Lady Padmore had taken to breakfasting downstairs instead of remaining in her room, and from the moment she entered the breakfast parlour the attacks began, and continued throughout the day.

That morning she was wearing an ugly sludge green and purple turban to cover her hair, which Miss Browne would spend an hour dressing later in the day, and an incongruously frivolous dressing gown with more tightly gathered gauze frills and ruffles of lace than she normally had on her evening gowns.

'If you do not obey me I will cancel your ball,' she said, as she lavishly buttered a roll.

Caroline looked startled. This threat had not been used before.

'It's Abby's ball as well. You can't stop it. She is paying for it.'

'Abigail can have her ball so long as she does nothing else to interfere with your concerns. I am sure Lady Jordan would be willing to come here and chaperon her while I take you back to Padmore Grange. Dudley will remain,' she added, casting a minatory glance at him.

He frowned. 'I can't stay here without any blunt. And who will pay the bills? You know Mr Wood insisted we didn't run up debts, and the pesky tradesmen have to be paid at once.'

'Lady Jordan will see to all that. It's none of your concern. Your next allowance is due in a week, and it's enough to manage on if you keep away from gaming hells and restrain your purchases of new clothes. You could sell that curricle and pair you bought last week if you need more.'

He frowned, but subsided. Abby was decidedly puzzled. Surely, if Lady Padmore left London, she would need Dudley's escort on the journey to Devon. She could not believe Dudley was needed in London. He had rarely escorted his mother and sister to social engagements, he refused to attend balls or go to Almack's, and without her presence he would undoubtedly revert to entertaining his disreputable friends in Hill Street, and coming home every night much the worse for drink. Lady Jordan would have no power to stop him, and she dreaded the resumption of his raucous parties disturbing their sleep.

Lady Padmore's voice interrupted Abby's thoughts.

'Well, Caroline? Are you going to be a sensible girl? I thought, as it is something you have expressed a wish for, we might pay a visit to Vauxhall if we remain here.'

Abby choked trying to suppress her laughter, and had to pretend she had swallowed a crumb the wrong way. How could Lady Padmore possibly believe such a treat would influence Caroline?

Caroline resisted, but the pressure grew. Only when Lady Padmore rose from the table and said she was going to instruct Miss Browne to pack their clothes, and ordered

Dudley to go and hire a post chaise for the following day, did Caroline succumb.

'I can't bear this! Oh, have your own way!' she cried, and rose unsteadily to her feet. Before she could reach the door Dudley had caught hold of her and forced her back into her chair, where her mother loomed over her.

'I knew you would see sense eventually.'

Lady Padmore preened, and Abby clamped her lips together.

'You will write him a letter straight away. I am not allowing you to change your mind. And if you think remaining here will allow you opportunities to meet the wretch in secret, disabuse yourself of the notion. Dudley will accompany you everywhere.'

★ ★ ★

An hour later, Caroline, her face streaked with tears, came to Abby's room. Abby had spent the intervening time devising plans for rescuing her friends from Lady Padmore's control, but apart from appealing to Lord Wantock, a plan which she instantly dismissed, since surely he would not interfere with their mother's decision, her only solution was to appoint herself as a go-between. Dudley might have been given the task of accompanying his sister, to prevent meetings, but he could not also accompany herself. Lady Padmore might seek to throw a rub in their way by insisting she remained with Caroline, or herself accompanying one of them, but if she recruited Anne as well something might be arranged.

'I had to do it,' Caroline said, as soon as she was in the room, and promptly burst into tears.

'You've written the letter?'

'Yes, and Mama wrote one too,' she managed through her convulsive sobbing. 'She showed it to me, and put it inside the same cover. It threatened poor Hartley with charges of suborning my affections, and enticing me away from my family. I didn't know there were such crimes.'

'I doubt if there are,' Abby said. 'If he took you away, perhaps she could do something, but it's no crime for him to admire you and ask you to marry him. Mr Wood will know.'

'She said if I told anyone outside the family, even Cousin Julian, she would still take me back to Devon. I'd have no chance of seeing him ever again, but at least in London she can't prevent him from attending functions where I go too. Unless I'm forbidden to go to any.'

'She can't do that if she wants to find you a husband.'

'She wants Cousin Julian to offer for me, but he won't.'

'Don't be in despair. I can meet Hartley, and so can Anne, and we can pass messages. Perhaps,' she added thoughtfully, 'they had better not be written down. Then we can deny them.'

Caroline still sobbed, but she tried to smile.

'You are such good friends. But when he receives the letter, he will think I have truly given him up. He may go straight back to Bath. There will be no opportunity for you to meet him.'

'I think Hartley has more determination than that. I would not be surprised to find he comes here immediately when he receives the letter, and demands to hear from you directly that you mean it. He knows your mama,' she added.

'I won't be allowed to see him.'

'That in itself will make him suspicious. Dry your eyes. It's too late for me to take Rusty to the Park in the hope of meeting Hartley there, but I can take him for a walk. She is not to know I'll be going to Berkeley Square to see Anne and ask her to meet Hartley tomorrow morning. Better still, I will write to him from her house and send the message by her footman. Has your mama decided when we are to go to Vauxhall?'

'Yes, tomorrow.'

'Then I can tell Hartley to be there too, and perhaps you will have a chance to speak to him, or at least see him.'

Abby slipped out of the house through the kitchens, retrieved a joyful Rusty from the stables, and went straight to Berkeley Square. The butler there was reluctant to admit Rusty until Anne appeared and insisted the dog was untied from the railings where Abby had been planning to leave him, and led the way into a conservatory at the back of the house.

She listened in horror to Abby's account of that morning.

'Oh, I should die if my parents behaved like that to me!'

'Thomas is more acceptable to them than Hartley is to Lady Padmore. But will you try to see Hartley tomorrow, if I am unable to be in the Park at the usual time? Tell him Caroline was forced, and why, but she still considers herself betrothed to him. Meanwhile, can I write a note to him to reassure him, and send it to his hotel?'

'Of course.'

Anne fetched her writing desk and Abby swiftly wrote her letter. A footman was summoned, and the note sent. Although Abby did not wish to be away from Hill

Street for too long, she waited for his return. Unfortunately, the man said, Mr Lennox had just left the hotel, in somewhat of a hurry, so there was no reply.

'I'd best go back. That's where he'll be.'

She hastened back along Hill Street, and saw Hartley standing by the front door. It was closed, and from his expression she decided he had been refused entry. She halted some distance away, for she did not wish anyone in the house to see her talking to him, and when he finally turned away and came towards her she beckoned him to follow her back into Berkeley Square. Once safely round the corner she swiftly explained what had happened.

'We're going to Vauxhall tomorrow night. There must be some opportunity there for talking to Caroline. But you must be discreet, or her mama will whisk her back to Devon, and it would be easier to lock her up there.'

Hartley paled. 'Surely even that she-devil would not do that?'

'Why not? Her venom and determination are strong. She may try to hurt you, or your reputation, if she thinks she cannot be rid of you any other way. Your uncles would not believe her, would they? And perhaps cut you out of the business so that your income falls?'

'Just let her try! They would believe me

first. But I'll be at Vauxhall. Will you take a box?'

'Of course. Lady Padmore will not wish to mingle with the common herd,' she said scornfully. 'As if many of them could afford three shillings and sixpence for admission! You will be able to see us, and after supper I will contrive somehow to detach Caroline. I don't know Vauxhall, so where could we meet?'

'I've never been there either, but I will ask my friends tonight, and tell you or Anne in the morning where we might meet safely.'

★   ★   ★

By rising especially early the following morning, Abby was able to escape to the Park with Rusty before Lady Padmore thought to forbid it. Caroline declared she dared not come, so Abby had to go alone, and while away the time before she might expect to see either Anne or Hartley.

It was an hour before Hartley appeared, and he looked heavy-eyed. He admitted he had slept little, but he had found someone who knew Vauxhall Gardens well.

'The South Walk is to the side of the Grand Walk, parallel to it. Tell Caroline I will wait for her just beyond the first archway. That will not be far for her to walk alone. But I hope you or Anne will be able to come with her. The best time will be just after nine o'clock, when everyone goes to watch the Cascade. I'm told it only lasts for fifteen minutes, and so Caroline ought to be able to lose the others in the crowd.'

'She will be safe if she keeps to the main walks, as I believe they are well lit. I had better try to distract Dudley and his mama.'

'Dudley will be there? Who else is going in your party?'

Abby frowned. 'The Crofts. Lady Padmore is trying to persuade me to show Harold favour. And Lord Wantock. She still wants him to offer for Caroline.'

'I thought he liked you?'

'So do I, but he won't offer for me. His family is far too important to be allied with a girl who does not even know who her parents' families were.'

She dressed for the visit with care. Even though nothing could come of the earl's interest in her, she knew he did like her, and she wanted to look her best. She had a new evening gown in pale green, embroidered round the neck and hem in silver thread, and with silver and dark green embroidery on the bodice. The pattern of this was repeated in narrow, elongated triangles falling from the bodice down the skirt. It was topped with a silver gauze overdress and she carried a dark green Paisley shawl Lady Jordan had bought for her. The necklace of malachite, a much darker green, glowed against her pale skin, and she dressed her hair so that a long ringlet fell over one shoulder while the rest was confined by a dark green ribbon edged with silver.

Caroline wore white.

'Most of the debutantes will be wearing white,' Abby pointed out. 'It will help to confuse Dudley if he attempts to pursue you.'

Lady Padmore had arranged for the earl and the Crofts to travel to the gardens together, while the four of them used her own carriage, but when they met in the Grove just past the entrance, Mrs Croft reported that Lord Wantock had sent his apologies, he was delayed, and would make his own way to Vauxhall.

For an hour they strolled along the gravel walks, and Caroline was able to identify the triumphal archway where Hartley would meet her. She confided to Abby that she felt certain he was already there and would be watching her while keeping safely out of sight. Abby devoutly hoped the last was true. She had no illusions. Lady Padmore, if she glimpsed him, was quite capable of whisking Caroline away to Devon at once.

Abby was enchanted with the gardens, the groves of trees, the tall elms bordering the main walks, the statues, the booths where they would later have supper, and all the other attractions, not least the music which she could hear when they were near the Grove, and watching the thousands of visitors parading to show off all their finery.

The only jarring note was the presence of Harold and Dudley. The latter had been unusually quiet for the past couple of days, even polite towards her. Harold appeared to have forgotten her scathing attack at the theatre. Both of them seemed determined to escort her, and she found herself flanked by them as they strolled. Was this of their own accord, or had Lady Padmore detailed Dudley, at least, to make sure the earl did not have any opportunities to pay her attentions?

Lady Padmore herself kept Caroline beside her, while Gregory escorted his mother. At last it was nine o'clock, and the crowd converged on the Cascade. Abby, saying she wanted to speak to Lady Padmore, drew her escort closer, and then pretended to stumble and fall against that lady. Both of them staggered, and Abby, seeming about to fall, clutched at Lady Padmore's arm. When they had righted themselves she saw with satisfaction that Caroline had vanished. With less satisfaction she saw Dudley darting away through the crowd, but she hoped he was not able to see where Caroline went.

Then all thoughts of Caroline left her as the earl appeared at her side.

★ ★ ★

Lord Wantock had been surprised on receiving Lady Padmore's invitation to join her party to Vauxhall Gardens, but when he arrived and saw how Harold Croft remained firmly at Abby's side, preventing him from talking privately with her, he began to suspect Lady Padmore's designs.

He glanced round. Caroline was not visible, nor her brother. He had not been able to ride in the Park since the evening at the theatre, and wanted to ask his cousin how matters stood now between herself and Hartley.

When the Cascade entertainment ended people moved back to their booths for supper. Lady Padmore began to fret about Caroline, but when Harold offered to go to look for her she refused.

'You must stay with Abigail. Gregory, perhaps you and Julian could go? Where is Dudley?'

'Perhaps they went together,' Abby suggested. 'It was rather a crush, and she may have been feeling faint.'

'They'll return in due time,' the earl said, making no attempt to leave. 'Do you realize how big the gardens are? It covers several acres, and how we might be expected to find one girl amongst the thousands of visitors tonight I cannot tell.'

'You always were disobliging!'

'They know where our supper booth is, they can find their way back there,' Abby said.

Lady Padmore was still railing at him, and he considered how repellent it made her look.

'You'd let my Caroline be abducted by that presumptuous merchant who wants to marry her?'

Abby was unable to remain silent at this slur on her friend.

'Hartley would never do such a thing! He is an honourable man. Merchants can be just as virtuous as the *ton*. More than some, I suppose, or they would not prosper for long if they didn't honour their debts, or cheated their customers!'

'That will do, Abigail! If there is any more impertinence from you I will send you home with Dudley.'

The earl smothered his grin as Abby, undaunted, shrugged.

'Where is he? I suspect he is searching some of the darker paths in the hope of finding the trollops who are reputed to haunt them.'

Lady Padmore visibly swelled, her face going red, and Mrs Croft tut-tutted loudly.

'You are an unprincipled chit. This is all your fault and I'm sorry I ever agreed to sponsor you.'

Seeing Abby open her mouth to respond, he decided it was time he intervened.

'Why do we not go to the supper booth? In all probability we will find at least one of the culprits there.'

Nobly, he considered, he took his cousin's arm and drew her away. Though she muttered angrily to herself all the way, and cast inimical glances at Abby, walking demurely beside Harold, she went with him. Caroline was sitting at the back of the booth, and she gave him a shy smile, then glanced swiftly at Abby and nodded slightly.

So something was afoot, he thought. He busied himself settling the older ladies at the front of the booth, keeping Lady Padmore as far from her daughter as possible. He thought she would not care to make a scene in such a public place, but did not feel inclined to depend on it. Many people were strolling past, some on their way to their own booths, others simply gazing at the more fortunate or wealthy visitors. They were barely settled when Dudley, in a raging temper, arrived.

'Where the devil did you go?' he demanded of Caroline, ignoring the interested glances of passers-by, some of whom had stopped at the sound of his raised voice and were watching, anticipating a fight.

'I strolled round, away from the crowds,' Caroline replied, and Julian was intrigued at how calm and composed his normally timid cousin appeared.

Abby had secured the seat next to her, and Julian managed to sit on her other side. They could not talk privately, but at least she was to some extent insulated from Dudley's anger.

He appeared to realize what an exhibition he was making of himself, and after glaring at the spectators, flung himself into the only vacant seat and began to help himself to the food. The others, after a few moments, also began to eat.

There was the famous ham, sliced so thinly it was possible to read a newspaper through it. There were chickens, cheesecakes and biscuits, and what Julian found was excellent wine as well as the potent arrack punch. Dudley was drinking the latter rather too freely, and Harold was attempting to persuade Abby to try it.

'No thank you,' Julian heard her say. 'I won't agree to dance the waltz with you when I am sober, and even if you succeed in making me drunk, which is unlikely, the answer is still no. Apart from every other consideration you're a very clumsy dancer.'

When they had all eaten, Lady Padmore, plastering a smile on her face, suggested that the two girls might like to stroll about the gardens again.

'Cousin Julian, I know I can trust you to make sure Caroline comes to no harm, and Dudley, you go with Abigail.'

The earl was highly amused and had to pretend to cough as he watched Harold's indignant face. Why was the Croft fellow making up to Abby? He needed to marry a fortune, and for the past two years had been pursuing every heiress to come to London. Had some rumour that she might be worth marrying been circulating amongst the younger fortune hunters? Lady Padmore's attitude was even more intriguing. He suspected she disliked Abby, tolerating her only because of the benefits acquired through her. Was she simply trying to divert Harold's interest, or promote her own son's?

Abby swiftly rose to her feet, pulling Caroline with her. She linked arms with her friend, and the two men perforce had to fall in to either side. All Dudley's attempts to draw Abby away failed. By the time they returned to the booth he was again in a barely concealed fury.

Lady Padmore was ready to leave. The Crofts made their farewells swiftly and departed. Harold was scarcely able to mutter thanks, and his glare at Dudley promised an interesting confrontation when next they met. Julian escorted them to the gates, and waited until their carriage was fetched. Then, remarking that he looked forward to seeing them at the ball in a few days' time, he left to find his own carriage.

12

The day of the ball came. Caroline was a little more cheerful because she knew Hartley would be there, and said her mother could not prevent her from dancing with him. Abby was not so confident. She had no illusions about that lady's aversion to a marriage with Hartley, or her determination, at whatever cost, to prevent the lovers from meeting.

Caroline, as usual, wore white. Her ballgown was trimmed with seed pearls, and embroidery in which Abby privately thought was an unfortunate insipid pink, and a multiplicity of pink bows and ribbons. Her cheeks glowed, however, at the prospect of seeing Hartley, and her eyes sparkled, so she did not look as colourless as usual.

Abby had chosen a very pale lilac sarsenet fabric, with short sleeves in blond lace. She resisted all Lady Padmore's attempts to add embellishments, and wore a simple ribbon of the same silk threaded through her curls. She also refused to wear her pearls, despite Lady Padmore's declaration that debutantes should not flaunt coloured jewels. Her amethysts echoed both the fabric and her eyes.

They were to dine at Wantock House. Abby had not been consulted on the guest list, but she was pleased to see both Lady Jordan and Mr Wood were present. Her trustee's presence, she assumed, had been at the earl's instigation, since she did not credit Lady Padmore with suggesting his name. She was less pleased to see the Croft brothers. Dudley had grudgingly agreed to grace the occasion with his presence, and Anne and her parents were also there.

The earl's sister and her husband were present, and Abby was puzzled by the cold glance with which Lady Jane greeted her. Had her curtsy not been deep enough, she wondered?

The countess's greeting was kind, and she complimented Abby on the charming simplicity of her gown. Abby could not resist a glance of triumph at Lady Padmore, but Caroline's mama was too busy talking to Lady Jane and glaring at Mr Wood to notice.

How had he offended her? How was Lady Jane involved, if she was?

Abby put these questions to the back of her mind. No doubt in time she would learn the answers. She was more anxious to talk to the earl. She had not seen him alone for some time, since the ride to Richmond. He was, as host, busy talking to the other guests, but eventually he came across the drawing room to speak to her.

'Abby, I have to start the ball with Caroline, but will you keep me the first waltz and the supper dance please?'

As she nodded she heard a gasp behind her. Glancing over her shoulder she saw Harold, gobbling like a stranded fish, she later told Anne. Fortunately, at that moment dinner was announced, and she was able to avoid him. He would, she was convinced, protest loudly that he had asked her first. He seemed oblivious to her snubs, as, lately, had Dudley been, and she was at a loss to wonder why their former attitude towards her had changed.

Afterwards she and Caroline had to stand with the countess, the earl, and Lady Padmore to greet the guests, but when the music started they were released. The earl bore Caroline off, and Mr Wood claimed Abby for the first dance, a quadrille.

'It's many years since I danced this,' he murmured to her as they stood watching the next couples perform the first figure. 'I trust I won't disgrace you.'

There was little time for further conversation, and it was inappropriate to discuss the situation between Caroline and Hartley, but Abby did obtain his promise to drive her on the following day. With that she had to be content. She could then ask his advice.

She saw Hartley enter the ballroom during the next dance, and stand half hidden behind a pillar. She hoped he would be able to approach Caroline before her mother could intervene.

Soon a waltz was announced, and the earl came to claim her. As they moved on to the floor she saw Hartley leading out Caroline, and silently applauded them both. She caught a glimpse of Lady Padmore, sitting on a sopha at the side of the room, and almost laughed at the look of chagrin on her face. Caroline would have to suffer later, she knew, but she had at least been able to dance and talk with Hartley.

'You seem distracted,' the earl said. 'Are you happy with the arrangements?'

Abby smiled up at him.

'The decorations are superb. Pink and lilac. How did you know the colours of our gowns?'

'I expect Lady Padmore told my mother. Cousin Hester has been here several times to oversee the preparations. What is the matter with her tonight? She looks as though she has swallowed a spider.'

Abby laughed. 'She hates Hartley being here. After she forced Caroline to break off her engagement, she thought they would not meet again.'

'She clearly did not take your determination into account. I like Lennox. He's a sensible fellow, though he's still young. He and Caroline will do well together.'

'Then you have no objection to their marriage?'

'If she is happy, that is all that matters. But enough of them,' he added, and suddenly swung her off the floor and into a small anteroom where chairs had been placed for people to sit out. Doors opened on to a balcony, and he drew her outside. The gardens were illuminated with dozens of lanterns, and already a few couples were strolling along the paths.

He led her down some steps on to the lawn, and into a small arbour covered with honeysuckle and rambling roses just beginning to show their colour. Abby sniffed appreciatively, but her heart was pounding. What was he intending?

He took both her hands in his, and she trembled at the contact. Then he unbuttoned her glove and raised her hand to his lips, kissing the inside of her wrist and making her tremble even more. He laughed a trifle unsteadily.

'This is not the best place, Abby, but I can

hope we will not be interrupted, and I cannot wait for a more propitious moment. I seem to have been waiting for months. Abby, my darling, I want you so badly. Will you marry me?'

* * *

The waltz ended, and Hartley was leading Caroline off the floor when Lady Padmore, with Dudley in tow, confronted them. Mr Wood was standing by the main entrance, a few yards away, but he clearly heard the venomous hiss as Lady Padmore ordered Hartley out of her sight and told Caroline they were going home directly if she could not behave herself with proper decorum and respect for her mother's orders.

Caroline, who had looked radiant a few moments before, burst into tears. Mr Wood moved swiftly towards the group and by taking both Lady Padmore's arm and Caroline's, managed to usher them out of the ballroom before many people had noticed the disturbance. Lady Padmore was too startled to object, and Mr Wood ignored the bleating coming from Dudley. He glanced back at Hartley and pointed to the door of the dining room, which was likely to be empty at this time. Hartley, after a brief hesitation, took the hint and removed himself. Mr Wood propelled Lady Padmore into a small parlour, and Caroline, sobbing wildly, followed and sank into a chair beside the fireplace. Dudley, stammering protests, was close behind her.

'Shut the door unless you want everyone to hear.'

Dudley obeyed, but uttered some inarticulate words which were ignored.

'My lady, whatever your private quarrels, you must not ruin Caroline's ball,' Mr Wood said sternly.

'She has disobeyed me, the wretched girl! I told her to have no more to do with that scoundrel!'

'That is your prerogative, but to create such a scandal at her ball is most ill-mannered.'

'Ill — ill-mannered! Sir, how dare you accuse me of that? You don't know what is proper behaviour, from what Dudley and Lady Jane have told me!'

'I hardly think your son is qualified to judge that, from what I have seen of his drunken antics at the East and West.'

'Oh, really! What of your own reputation?' Dudley managed to say, but his voice trembled.

Mr Wood looked at him for a long moment, and Dudley turned a fiery red, then threw himself into a chair.

'My manners and reputation are not the issue here.' He turned back to Lady Padmore, who was standing facing him. 'I am beginning to believe I chose the wrong person to sponsor Miss Barton into the *ton*.'

He watched her bite back the retort on her tongue. She went pale under her cosmetics, and seemed to have difficulty breathing.

'What do you mean?' she whispered, reaching behind her for a chair.

Mr Wood pushed one towards her and she sank into it, clutching her heart.

'I can cancel the lease on the house, and give orders no more of your bills will be paid by me. What will your acquaintances say when I remove Abby from your care and find another chaperon for her, in the middle of the Season? There will be speculation, and gossip. I've no doubt that bitter tongue of yours has made you some enemies, and they will gloat unmercifully.'

'You wouldn't dare! Any gossip would harm Abigail too.'

'I doubt it. I have the means of letting people know the truth. And they will believe me.'

There was silence apart from Caroline's sobs and Lady Padmore's heavy breathing. Mr Wood looked at her and sat down opposite.

'My lady, you have the right of a parent to refuse to allow Caroline's betrothal, I do not dispute that. If you can behave with proper restraint towards her for the rest of the evening, I will say no more. But Mr Lennox is here as Abigail's guest, you will not turn him away. I will ensure he does not dance with Caroline again, but he is to be allowed to remain. Are you agreed?'

She had difficulty suppressing her desire to argue, but eventually she nodded. Mr Wood turned to Dudley.

'Can I trust you to behave properly as well?'

Dudley nodded grudgingly. 'I have to, if Mama says so.'

'Then do something useful for your sister. Go and find Abby, or young Anne Quinton, and ask them to come here to Caroline. She must go back if we are to stifle speculation. My lady, you may leave Caroline with me. I'll see she is able to return soon.'

Lady Padmore had barely left the room before Anne entered. She ran across to Caroline and provoked a fresh burst of weeping by asking what had happened.

'Miss Quinton, can I depend on you to help Caroline repair the damage to her face and come back to the ball? Don't upset her with questions. Just say she felt faint if anyone asks.'

'Of course I'll help her.'

He turned to Caroline, who had ceased weeping.

'I'll see young Lennox and tell him you are feeling better, but he must not provoke your mama again by talking to you.'

'Thank you, sir,' Caroline managed.

He gave both girls an encouraging smile and left the room.

* * *

Abby clung to the earl, breathing hard. His kisses had robbed her of breath, and she was smiling and laughing.

'You can't mean it,' she gasped. 'I'm a nobody, I have no family, I don't even know who my parents were, and I'm not rich.'

'What do any of those things matter if we love one another? Abby, you haven't said you love me. Have I mistaken your feelings?'

'No, no, of course not. But your family, they will be horrified. They want you to make a good match.'

'Jane is rather top lofty, but my mother will happily accept any girl I love, and we don't have to see Jane very often.'

'She was looking furious when I arrived. Do you think she has guessed, and that accounts for her scowls?'

'I cannot recall a single day when Jane has not been scowling over something, or disapproving of what I have done or not done. I may be the nominal head of the family, but that does not prevent her from scolding me or telling me what to do. Enough of her. When shall we be married, and where? Do you wish to be married in Bath? How long will it take you to purchase your bride clothes? Could we be wed in July, and I can take you to Paris and Italy?'

Abby was laughing.

'Stop, stop! I haven't even thought of these things.'

'I'll go to see Mr Wood in the morning. He will have to give his consent, I suppose. Is he your guardian?'

'He's my trustee. I don't think I have a guardian, unless it's Aunt Emily. She has never said.'

'We'll sort that out. Come here, I want to kiss you again. When shall we tell people? Tonight? I could ask Mr Wood straight away. Shall we have a grand announcement at supper?'

'Please, no!'

'Are you ashamed of me?'

'Of course not. It's Caroline. She'd feel it badly, after what has happened to her. Let me tell her privately.'

'Then we can have another party to

225

celebrate, with just a few of our real friends.'

'Ought we to go back now? Surely we will be missed. It must be almost time for supper.'

Reluctantly she drew away from him, but they both found it difficult to separate, and it was some time later before they returned to the ballroom. Julian slipped away, but Abby knew her glow of happiness would alert the people she knew best that something had happened to her. She schooled her smiles and took a deep breath as she prepared to face everyone.

The first person she encountered as she came through the doorway was Anne, looking worried.

Abby stopped. 'What is it?'

'That nasty old witch began to make a fuss about Caroline and Hartley dancing together. Caroline was devastated.'

Abby's bubble of happiness burst.

'Where is she?'

'Upstairs, in one of the bedrooms. Mr Wood got them out of the ballroom before the row was noticed, and Lady Padmore and Dudley went back in. He, Mr Wood, asked me to help Caroline, and I was just taking her to wash her face when the countess saw us. She knew at once something was upsetting her, and took her upstairs. I hope it doesn't set her off crying again, or she'll never get the redness out of her eyes.'

'How long is it to supper?'

'Another country dance after this one. Half an hour, perhaps.'

'Where is Mr Wood?'

'I don't know. He went to talk to Hartley, but I haven't seen him either. He made Caroline promise not to speak to him again this evening, so I suppose he's gone to tell Hartley the same. Caroline didn't tell me what he said to her mama, but she was looking shattered when I saw her going back into the ballroom. I was going to Caroline.'

The next dance began, and Anne was claimed by Thomas, her partner.

'Caroline will be all right with the countess,' she whispered to Abby as she allowed him to lead her into the set.

Julian then arrived, and Abby swiftly told him what she had learned. There was no opportunity to talk as the movements of the dance separated them repeatedly. Abby watched for Hartley and Mr Wood, but saw neither of them return to the ballroom. Then it was time for supper.

★ ★ ★

The remainder of the ball passed without further incident. Caroline returned, pale but composed, and Abby noticed how the countess took pains to be beside her in the intervals between dances. Hartley had vanished, and Abby assumed he did not wish to cause Caroline extra distress by being in the same room but unable to speak to her. Mr Wood had not returned, and when Julian managed to speak to Abby towards the end of the ball, before the last set of dances, he told her that there had been a message about some problem which had arisen, causing Mr Wood to leave early.

Both Harold and Dudley solicited Abby for dances, but her card had been filled early in the evening, and she was relieved to be able to deny them. She was quite happy to say she did not wish to dance with them, but accepted that if she had denied them and then not had a partner they would feel even more aggrieved than they did already. Soon afterwards both Dudley and Harold left the ball, and Abby assumed they had gone on to more exciting entertainments.

Lady Padmore attacked her on the short drive home.

'Dudley tells me you refused to dance with him. Surely, as he is your host, you could have spared him one dance.'

'And which of my partners, to whom I had already promised dances, should I have offended? Besides, I don't consider him in any way my host. He was not involved in your negotiations with Mr Wood, nor would he have been here if he had had the courage to continue in the army. In fact,' she added thoughtfully, 'if Mr Wood had seen him I suspect he would have looked for a different chaperon.'

For a few moments Lady Padmore was unable to speak, merely taking deep breaths.

'Impertinence! Never mind quibbling. You gave Lord Wantock two dances. There were comments about that, when he only danced once with Caroline, who is his cousin.'

'I am hardly to be held responsible for his lordship's actions,' Abby said, secretly hugging to herself the knowledge that soon Lady Padmore would have even more to complain about when she heard of the engagement.

They arrived home soon afterwards, and the girls escaped to their rooms. Caroline, after ensuring her mother was in her own bedroom, and not intending to berate her again for dancing with Hartley, went into Abby's room and told her all that had happened. She was inclined to weep, and was anxious, but told the story clearly.

'Mr Wood was wonderful! If he had not rescued me I should have made such a spectacle of myself in the ballroom. But where did Hartley go?'

'I expect he thought it better not to inflame your mama even more by being seen in the ballroom. But either Anne or I will meet him soon, and discover what he means to do.'

'She'll never permit us to marry!'

'Let's wait and see. Don't allow her to force you into a betrothal to anyone else.'

'She's determined to make Julian marry me. And though I like him, and he's always kind, I don't love him, and he doesn't love me.'

Abby took a deep breath. Now was the time for her own confession.

'She won't be able to,' she said slowly.

Caroline looked at her, and then a smile transformed her doleful expression.

'Abby, you don't mean — '

Abby nodded. 'Yes, he's asked me to marry him! He'll go and see Mr Wood tomorrow, and then we can announce it!'

Caroline gave a squeal of excitement and hugged Abby convulsively.

'Abby, oh, how wonderful! You and Julian to marry! You'll be my cousin!'

They both started when the bedroom door opened, and Lady Padmore, garbed in her dressing gown, stepped into the room.

'So that's what you have been scheming for, is it, you deceitful jade! I knew I was harbouring a snake in the grass. We'll soon see about that. I doubt the countess will approve of her son marrying a nameless hussy with no fortune and no family apart from a rascally trustee passing himself off as a respectable businessman, whose business dealings are as shady as he is himself.'

13

When Abby descended to a late breakfast she found Caroline, red-eyed, and Lady Padmore frowning. The latter barely nodded to her.

Abby helped herself to tea and toast from the sideboard and sat down. There were two letters beside her plate. One was in Mr Wood's writing and she opened it first.

He explained he was forced to go out of Town, and apologized for being unable to drive her out that afternoon. He would come and see her the moment he returned.

Curious about the other, in an elegant but unknown hand, she broke the seal and read, then began to smile.

'What is it?' Lady Padmore broke her silence to demand.

Abby looked at her, unable to keep the look of pleasure from her face.

'Lady Wantock. A most affectionate note. She wishes to see me and I am invited to tea this afternoon. Lord Wantock is calling for me.'

'Humph! Show it to me.'

'What right do you have to inspect my correspondence? I have told you the contents, but I don't feel you have any right even to ask for that.'

'As your chaperon, my girl, I have every right to make sure you are not engaged in any dubious activities.'

Abby laughed, and handed her the note.

'I don't think even you, my lady, could object to an invitation to tea from my future mother-in-law! As for calling it a dubious activity, I suppose that is your privilege.'

Lady Padmore read the note several times, then laid it down beside her plate.

'You may think this an affectionate note, but I read it differently. It is merely polite. I suspect she is going to tell you such a marriage with her son is out of the question. There are far more eligible girls he can marry, including my own daughter.'

'I don't wish to marry him!' Caroline said, and another tear ran slowly down her cheek.

Abby broke off a piece of toast and took a deep breath before she spoke. She bit back her first impulse to say exactly what she thought of Lady Padmore's character. It would hurt Caroline, however much at odds the girl now was with her mother.

'Perhaps you should listen to Caroline and accept her wishes. As for me, you hope it is the case the countess will not accept me, but you are blinded by your prejudice. Julian is not under his mother's control, he can marry where he wishes.'

'He is a dutiful son, and will take her advice. Caroline, be ready in half an hour. We have a fitting for your new ballgown. It is Anne Quinton's ball next week, and I wish you to look your best. The Season is more than half done.'

Caroline rose obediently, and Abby followed her.

'Mama may say she still hopes Cousin Julian will offer for me, but I think she is starting to accept it will not happen. She is casting about for another suitor, and has little time left,' Caroline said, as they reached the privacy of her room. 'She won't be able to afford another Season for me unless she can persuade someone else to pay her, as Mr Wood has for you.'

'Then she may come to accept Hartley as a last resort,' Abby said.

Caroline chuckled. 'He's my first resort! But I hate the thought of having to wait, perhaps for two or three years. And he might meet someone else.'

'He won't desert you. He loves you. And I've known him all my life. Once he makes up his mind nothing can sway him. Now get ready. Your mama has not yet thought to forbid me to go out, so I will take Rusty for a walk and try to speak to Hartley at his hotel.'

'Abby, you ought not to visit a man at his hotel!'

'I won't. I'll just send a message for him to come out if he is there. They won't permit Rusty inside, so you need not fear for my reputation. Now do get ready, before your mama remembers me. I think, just in case she does, I will slip out now. If she asks where I am you don't know.'

★ ★ ★

'The man is a card sharp! How can you propose demeaning yourself and mortifying your family by an alliance with someone connected to him? I imagine the money that is paying for her Season comes from the fortunes he has won — or worse — from gullible young fools!'

Julian looked at his sister with dislike, and wondered how she came to be so discontented and vindictive. Was it because she had herself married, not for love, but for the immense fortune her husband was expected to inherit? Unfortunately for Jane his elderly Nabob godfather, though prevented from many activities since losing a leg many years ago in India, still enjoyed life as far as he was able, entertaining his raffish friends lavishly

235

either in London or one of his country estates. The fortune, Julian had heard, was fast disappearing as he insisted on presenting these friends, and a varied collection of ladies whose favours he had enjoyed in the past, with embarrassingly expensive tokens of his esteem. He had heard the sum of £10,000 a year spent at Rundell and Bridge on various items of jewellery, and several of the ladies as well as the men friends had acquired carriages and horseflesh, even houses, they could not have afforded on what Julian knew were limited incomes. Crates of the best wine, indeed, appeared regularly at Wantock House, and no doubt elsewhere, and Jane complained bitterly that he did not need the wine, and neither did any of the other dozen or more recipients of such bounty she knew about. Julian, who rather liked the old reprobate, knew there were far more than a dozen people who enjoyed this generosity.

'Mr Wood is no card sharp, and I advise you not to call him that if you do not wish to be charged with slander. He is a respected businessman in the City.'

'He owns a gambling establishment, the East and West. Why, it is but a few doors away from his own house.'

'Does he, indeed? I wasn't aware of that. If

it is true he has one of the best chefs in Town there, almost as good as Watier's.'

'Of course it's true! My friend Harold Croft discovered it from one of the men who works there. Don't you care?'

'I cannot see that the ownership of a club is any more reprehensible than the ownership of racehorses. Both involve gambling.'

Jane flushed. 'How dare you compare Ilroy's hobby with an establishment where young men are encouraged to lose fortunes?'

'I merely point out that gambling exists in many forms. If men hazard what they cannot afford on horse racing, do you blame your husband for providing the horses?'

'It is not at all the same. He's an upstart. No one knows where he came from. Neither do they know where this chit belongs. None of the Barton families I know can have any connection with her. I suspect she is Wood's bastard, and he is attempting to foist her on Society.'

'If she is, she can scarcely be held responsible. I wonder,' he added, smothering a grin, 'how many bastards are accepted because their mothers happen to be respectably married? Or not, if they live in Devonshire House.'

'What they do is of no importance to me. We have always been a respectable family, and this girl and Wood are not at all respectable.'

'That is your opinion, for which you have absolutely no justification.'

'I'm older than you, Julian, I know more of the world, and I think you ought to listen to my advice.'

He laughed. 'Jane, I am eight and twenty, old enough to know my own mind, and I am determined to marry Abby. You have been urging me to wed for years, and provide an heir, and now I propose to do just that you are objecting. Pray excuse me, I have to go to her now and bring her to meet Mama.'

'We'll see about that,' he heard her mutter as he picked up his hat and left the room.

He sighed. The countess, he knew, would welcome his intended bride, but Jane could make life uncomfortable for Abby if she maintained her unreasonable hostility. Then he grinned. Abby, he felt sure, would not be deterred, and he foresaw some lively confrontations in which, he suspected, his sister would be routed.

★ ★ ★

Caroline returned from her fitting and hurried up to Abby's bedroom.

'Did you see him?' she demanded.

Abby nodded. 'Yes, and he means to remain in London. He hopes you may meet in the Park when we take our morning walks there.'

'If Mama permits them.'

'She cannot prevent his attending balls or the theatre, and even if she manages to ensure you don't speak, you can look at one another.'

'She still has hopes of Cousin Julian.'

Abby looked at her in astonishment.

'How can she, when he is betrothed to me?'

'She was talking to Dudley, in the drawing room, before we went out. I listened outside the door, it wasn't closed.'

'What are they plotting?'

'She still does not believe the countess will accept you. Abby, Dudley told her Mr Wood owns a gambling club, I think he called it the East and West. He said Julian would not wish to be connected to it, and Mama should inform him of it.'

'A club? Like White's? How exciting! Can ladies go there? I've always longed to see what happens.'

Caroline laughed. 'Abby! How can you? I don't think ladies are permitted to gamble in public clubs, only at private parties.'

'Does Julian know?'

'My dear brother didn't say. I was only there for a moment, and then Miss Browne came along and I had to go in.'

'I'll tell him when he calls for me. How do I look? I have to make a good impression with his mama.'

She was wearing a simple walking gown in a delicate shade of green, with darker green lace flounces round the hem, a straw bonnet with floating green ribbons, and a new pelisse in a shade which almost matched her hair.

'An ideal attire for visiting one's new mama. It's discreet but attractive. When is Cousin Julian coming?'

'In a few minutes. I must go downstairs.'

She had reached the next landing when a knock came on the front door, so she went straight down to the hall as the butler admitted Julian.

He came to her and took both hands in his.

'You look enchanting,' he said, and Abby heard a slight catch in his voice. 'Are you ready?'

'Yes. Julian. I have to tell you something, but not here. Let us go. I can tell you on the way. Do we walk, or have you brought your carriage?'

'I thought you would not object to walking. The day is pleasant, and it gives us more time together. Is Lady Padmore in? I should pay my respects.'

'No, please don't. I'll explain. Come, we

must go before she realizes you are here.'

Although Abby had entertained no fears that Julian would despise her for Mr Wood's connection with gambling, she was not so confident his mother would not object. She had tried to appear unconcerned when talking to Caroline, but a slight niggle of doubt remained.

'What is it?' he asked, as soon as they were outside the house. 'You sound nervous. There's no need, my mama will welcome you.'

'Perhaps not when she knows. Julian, I have just heard that Mr Wood is the owner of the East and West. It's a gambling club. Do you know it? Will your mother object to the connection?'

'I know, and I suspect my dear sister will by now have informed Mama. She was assaulting my ear with her objections before I came for you. But my love, how can it affect us? It's a very respectable club, and many men go there because Mr Wood employs an excellent chef. It has nothing to do with Jane or Mama, and whatever Jane is, Mama is not so unreasonable as to blame you for something which is nothing to do with you.'

'Is there blame in owning such an establishment?'

'Of course not. It is a simple business matter.'

Lady Jane was sitting with the countess when Abby was shown into a small parlour at the back of the Grosvenor Square house, and one glance at her informed Abby that here she had an implacable opponent. She glanced apprehensively towards the countess, who beckoned her closer.

'Come my dear, and let me kiss my new daughter. We were unable to say much last night, but I do hope you enjoyed your ball. I want to get to know you much better now. Sit here beside me and tell me all about yourself. You live in Bath, I hear, with Emily Jordan? I knew her many years ago, and was pleased to have a chat with her last night. She is coming to see me tomorrow, and I am hoping to persuade her not to return to Bath before we have had an opportunity to present you to all our friends.'

★　★　★

Abby, in a glow of happiness at the countess's welcome, was able to ignore Lady Padmore's bitter comments during the next few days. Julian loved her; his mother approved of her; Mr Wood, who had returned to London, had given his whole-hearted approval, and Julian had given her not only the family betrothal ring, a large emerald in antique setting, but a

242

parure of emeralds to match.

'We cannot have a betrothal party until after the Quinton ball,' the countess told her. 'Start to think how many guests you want to invite.'

She prepared for Anne's ball in somewhat of a daze. She had escaped from the house early one morning and spoken to Hartley, even though Caroline had been forbidden to walk in the Park without Dudley. She was able to reassure her friend he was constant in his affections, and tell her Julian meant to talk to Lady Padmore when that lady's ire had been given time to subside. To that end, and to avoid aggravating her animosity, he and Hartley had decided it would not be politic for Hartley to attend Anne's ball.

Caroline was disappointed but resigned. She had faith in Julian, and he had told her his mother would also be speaking to Lady Padmore. Meanwhile, Hartley was in correspondence with his uncles to establish exactly what his fortune consisted of, and what profits in the business he could expect in the future.

'We are increasing our business, especially now the wars are over and it is easier to trade with France,' he told Julian, but he did not yet have any exact estimate of what he might expect as income.

Abby decided to wear a white ballgown, which she had already worn at Almack's, as it was the most appropriate for showing off Julian's emeralds. It was of silk, and fortuitously embroidered all over the bodice in pale green. At the hem were flounces of alternating pale and dark green. Julian sent her a single red rose which she pinned to the bodice. He had also sent Caroline a pale pink rose, with a note that it was on Hartley's behalf.

When they arrived in Berkeley Square Julian was waiting for them and promptly bore Abby away to introduce her to his own friends. Her card was full within minutes, and Julian complained he had almost missed obtaining a waltz with her.

'You can waltz all you choose, and in private, once you are leg-shackled,' one of his friends, a cavalry officer, told him, and Abby blushed and grinned back.

Caroline, she was glad to see, was also dancing every dance. Some of her partners were the men Julian had introduced her to, and she suspected he had also introduced them to Caroline. Lady Padmore, perhaps unaware of this manoeuvre, was preening at her daughter's success, probably imagining another suitor might appear and oust Hartley from Caroline's affections. Now she had accepted she had lost any chance of snaring Julian she was clearly surveying other options.

It was during a rather lively quadrille that someone caught his foot in one of Abby's flounces, and as soon as the dance finished she retired to a small bedroom set aside for ladies to pin it up.

Lady Quinton's own maid was there, equipped with pins and needle and thread to deal with such emergencies, and she insisted it would only take a few minutes to repair the gown properly.

'You don't want it to fall down again, or a pin to stick in someone,' she said, and Abby laughed and submitted.

It did take only a few minutes, and the music for the next country dance was striking up as Abby went back downstairs. She hoped her partner, one of Julian's friends, had not given her up when he had been unable to find her.

The staircase was broad and swept round in a gentle curve. Abby was about halfway down when she noticed an elderly lady standing at the bottom, clutching the balustrade as she gazed up at Abby. She looked pale and began to sway, and Abby feared she was about to faint. She ran down the remaining stairs and took hold of the lady's arm to steady her.

'Ma'am, are you feeling unwell? Can I help you? Come, sit down for a moment, and if you have anyone here I can send for, I will do that.'

'Help me into the anteroom by the front door,' the lady said, clutching Abby's hand. 'Pray, don't let us disturb anyone. I shall be well enough in a few minutes.'

'Can I send for something? Water, or brandy?'

She shook her head. 'I have a vinaigrette in my reticule. That will restore me.'

With Abby's arm round her waist supporting her they reached the anteroom, and with a sigh the lady subsided onto a sopha.

'Please, child, will you shut the door? I have no desire to advertise my weakness.'

Abby did so, and returned to find the lady leaning back on the sopha, a small vinaigrette clutched in her hand.

'Are you sure I can do nothing to help, fetch no one?'

'Please, no. But stay and talk to me for a moment. Unless I am taking you away from some special beau you want to dance with?'

Abby disclaimed. She had only met her partner tonight, and Julian could explain to him. He knew about her torn flounce, and they might think she was still upstairs repairing it.

The lady sat up, looking much better. Colour had returned to her cheeks, and she had an intent look in her faded blue eyes. She was, Abby judged, in her sixties, but she was upright and, now she had recovered from her momentary indisposition, looked alert.

'What is your name?' she asked.

'Abigail Barton, ma'am.'

'Barton? And your family?'

'I have none. My parents both died before I was two years old, and I was brought up by Lady Jordan, in Bath.'

'Is she your guardian? Is she bringing you out?'

'I really don't know who my guardians are. No, she lives retired, and Lady Padmore is bringing me out with her own daughter, Caroline.'

'Padmore? Yes, I believe I have heard the name. Do they have a house in London? I come here so seldom and do not now go much into company, I have lost track of people, but Lady Quinton is the daughter of a very dear friend, and she persuaded me to come to Anne's ball tonight.'

'We stay in Hill Street,' Abby said, wondering at the lady's curiosity, and her apparent eagerness to explain herself.

'I see you are betrothed,' she said, picking up Abby's hand and touching the ring.

Her hand trembled, and Abby wondered if she was still feeling faint, but she did not appear about to swoon again.

'Yes, ma'am, to Lord Wantock.'

'Julian? He's found someone at last? He's been the despair of many young girls. I'm Lady Catherine Simon. My husband is now too frail to visit London, and remains in our house in Gloucestershire. Which is another reason I rarely come myself.'

'I'm sorry to hear about that.'

'You're a kind girl. Run along now, I am much better, and do not wish to keep you away from the dancing.'

'Can I not fetch someone, a friend?'

'Just tell Lady Quinton where I am, if you would be so kind. If I do not reappear soon she can come and find me.'

14

On the following afternoon Abby and Caroline were with Lady Padmore, dutifully awaiting callers. It was the usual day for Lady Padmore receiving, but while they waited for the first callers she was asking Caroline about her partners the previous evening.

Abby had difficulty in suppressing her amusement. At every name mentioned Lady Padmore would consult her memory and dredge up all the facts she could about the man, his family, his prospects and his current fortune. If he had, during the earlier part of the season, been paying attentions to other girls, she would speculate on how serious these attentions were, whether the girls involved had other admirers, and the likelihood of them accepting any offers made.

Caroline was struggling. Her mother had secured her dance card, and was grumbling at the difficulty in deciphering some of the names, sometimes just initials, written on it. Many of the men Caroline had not previously met, as they had been introduced that evening by Julian, and when she could remember no details of their conversations, or confused one with another, Lady Padmore was scathing in her condemnation of Caroline's memory and lack of interest.

'Do you not wish to receive an eligible offer?'

'I have already accepted one,' Caroline said.

She was obviously finding this inquisition both painful and irritating, and Abby was relieved when the first callers were announced.

Soon the drawing room was full and the maids busy handing round cups of tea and small cakes. Several of Caroline's partners from last night had come, and Lady Padmore was fulsomely gracious to them. If any of them were interested in Caroline her manner would be enough to deter them from wishing to become part of her family, Abby thought. Fortunately Hartley was strong and deeply in love with Caroline. He would be able to deal with her if she ever became his mother-in-law, and Abby promised herself to do all in her power to bring this about.

A couple of the young men were taking their leave when a newcomer was announced, and Abby looked up in astonishment. It was Lady Catherine Simon. Abby wondered whether she had come to thank her for her assistance the previous evening, but after a smile in Abby's direction she permitted Lady

Padmore, who had risen to greet her, to guide her to a seat beside that lady.

Abby was too far away to hear what was being said, but from the puzzled glances Lady Padmore cast in her direction she assumed she was the subject of their conversation. When two of the ladies were taking their leave of Lady Padmore she made an opportunity to approach Lady Catherine and ask her if she felt better now.

'Yes, my dear. I have to thank you for last night, you were very kind. Now, let me come and sit beside you and we can talk comfortably.'

From the look of irritation Lady Padmore gave Abby, it was clear she was not happy with this development, but there was nothing she could do about it. Abby had not mentioned the incident, and she expected to be taken to task later, accused of trying to keep the acquaintance to herself.

Lady Catherine sat down on a sopha near the window and patted the seat beside her.

'Come, my dear, sit beside me. I understand Lady Padmore is bringing you out. Is she an old friend of your family?'

'I have no family, ma'am. It was convenient for Lady Padmore to introduce me to Society at the same time as she brought out her own daughter.'

'But you do not normally live with her?'

'No. I live in Bath with Lady Jordan, but as she rarely comes to London she did not feel able to present me. She does not know all the right people, she says.'

'Is she your guardian?'

'I suppose I must have guardians, but I have never wondered who they are. That must seem strange to you, my lady, but I have never thought about it. Mr Wood is my trustee, and he may be a guardian too.'

'Mr Wood?'

Lady Catherine's question was sharp, abrupt, and when Abby looked at her in puzzlement she laughed and said she wondered if it was the Mr Wood she knew.

'Though it is a fairly common name, I suppose. Where does this trustee live? Is he an attorney?'

'He has a house in St James's Square, and offices in the City, and I believe he deals in the stock market. Is that the man you know?'

'Possibly. It may be. Tell me, child, did you enjoy the ball last night?'

'Very much, thank you.'

'Your own ball was a week ago, I understand. At Lord Wantock's house. Were you betrothed to him? Is that why you used his house? I am sorry I missed it.'

Abby was puzzled at all these questions,

but she decided it was just the curiosity of an old woman.

'Julian, Lord Wantock, is some sort of cousin to Lady Padmore, and that is why his house was used. He — ' She stopped and felt her cheeks grow warm. 'He actually asked me to marry him that evening.'

'How romantic. From all I hear he is an estimable young man. You are fortunate, but I believe he is even more so. Now, my dear, I must take my leave. I hope we will meet again soon while I am still in Town.'

★　★　★

The last of the visitors was leaving when Julian was announced. Lady Padmore frowned, and for a few moments Abby thought she was about to deny him, but she shrugged, turned back into the room and sat down facing the doorway.

He came in, smiled at Abby, and crossed to take her hands in his.

'How are you, my love? Not too tired after last night?'

She shook her head, and he turned to Lady Padmore.

'Cousin Hester, you are well?'

'I doubt you care! You have never listened to my advice, or my wishes, so it is rather hypocritical of you to start being concerned with my health.'

He pursed his lips but kept his voice level.

'I have some news for you, and wished to ensure that the shock would not bring on a seizure.'

'You need not be afraid of that. I am considered particularly robust in health, and this Season I think I have endured several shocks already. Well, say what you have to say?'

'May I sit down?' he asked, and without waiting for her reply sat beside Abby, where Lady Catherine had so recently been.

Before she could speak Dudley came into the room.

'Are they all gone?' he asked, and then saw Julian. 'Oh, you're here. What do you want?'

'I was about to tell your mother, but I am glad the whole family is here to have the information at once. It would be tedious to have to repeat it. I have just come from speaking to Mr Lennox.'

'That scoundrel! Is he trying to get you to intervene on his behalf?'

'I should have made it plainer. I meant the senior Mr Lennox, Hartley's uncle, the head of the firm he belongs to.'

'Well, he need not think he can make me change my mind and permit his nephew to ally himself with my family!'

'He came to me in the hope I might be able to soften your opposition,' Julian said, and Abby almost choked trying to smother her laughter.

'A futile hope. If that is all you have to say, Cousin, you can go and tell him I stand by my refusal to countenance a betrothal between his nephew and Caroline.'

'Then you don't wish her to have an income of, at a conservative estimate, twenty thousand a year?'

Lady Padmore's eyes grew round. Caroline gasped, and Dudley frowned and then sneered.

'A hum!' Dudley said. 'Don't let him fool you, Mama. How can that merchant possibly have such a fortune?'

'Easily, if he is a partner in a flourishing business, and his maternal grandfather brought back a fortune from India and left it to his only grandson when he came of age, which will be in a month's time. It is the difficulty in calculating the exact profits of the firm that makes the total sum vary by a thousand or so.'

Abby was grinning broadly.

'Did Hartley know?' she asked.

'Not the extent of the fortune, just that he would inherit something when he was of age.'

'It's more than your income!' Lady Padmore said, her voice faint, reaching into her reticule and bringing out a vinaigrette, something Abby had rarely seen her use. She must be really shattered at this news.

'Indeed, so apart from the lack of a title, I really do think Caroline would benefit if she married him.'

In considerable amusement Abby watched Lady Padmore struggle with her emotions. She had learned how inflexible Caroline's mama was, how convinced she was that she and she only was in the right. After her continuous and vociferous opposition to Hartley's suit she would have great difficulty in allowing herself to change her mind. Twenty thousand pounds a year, however, was a big incentive.

She glanced at Caroline, who was looking almost as devastated as her mama.

Julian spoke again, looking at Abby and taking her hand in his own.

'Hartley and his uncle are at Wantock House. They did not wish to intrude on you here until you had been apprised of the situation. I have suggested that I take you and Caroline there to meet them, in the event that you are prepared to agree to an engagement.'

'You'll need a lawyer to make sure they are not conning you!' Dudley said, glaring at

Julian. 'And as head of the family I want to make sure we are not being cheated!'

Abby laughed. 'A fine head of the family you make,' she said, then looked apologetically at Julian, and saw he was suppressing a smile.

'I think, Dudley, you can depend on me to look after Caroline's interests. You may be head of this family, but you are lacking in both knowledge of the world and common sense. I have rather more experience than you, and have already discussed terms of the settlements proposed, and they are generous.'

Abby somehow knew Dudley was longing to ask whether any of this largesse would devolve upon him, and she determined to speak to Hartley as soon as she could and advise against giving Dudley anything. No doubt he would provide something for Lady Padmore, but she hoped he would do it in a way that prevented Dudley from spending it on his own dubious activities.

'Well, Cousin? Do you withdraw all opposition to a marriage between Caroline and Hartley Lennox?'

It sounded, Abby thought a little hysterically, like the wedding service. Do you, Lady Hester, take this man to be your lawful wedded son-in-law?

There was a long pause, and Caroline looked imploringly at her mother.

'Mama, I love Hartley, I don't care about the money!'

'Don't care?' Lady Padmore almost shrieked. 'You foolish girl! Come, get your hat, we must go at once to Wantock House and see what sort of a trick they are playing.'

'Mama wishes us all to dine, if all goes well, and I can see it will, Cousin Hester, so perhaps you would prefer to change now to avoid having to come back?'

★ ★ ★

Mr Wood closed his eyes as his butler asked if he was at home to the lady who had just called and wished to see him on a matter of business. He had been afraid something like this might happen, but had depended on Lady Catherine's infrequent visits to London. It was not something he could avoid, and he had to face it.

'Show her into the drawing room. I will be with her in a few moments.'

He needed a short time to recover from this unexpected development, and consider how much to reveal, but he soon went upstairs. Lady Catherine was standing before the window, looking out across the square.

She turned as he shut the door and leaned back against it.

'So it is you,' she said softly. 'You have changed.'

'I am twenty years older, my lady. Won't you sit down? May I offer you something?'

She smiled faintly as she walked across the room and sank into a chair.

'Nothing, I thank you. You were not at the Quinton ball two nights ago, I think.'

'I was out of Town.'

'I met Abigail Barton. She is so like her mother, I thought for a moment my daughter had come back to life. But why the name Barton? You did marry my Abigail, did you not?'

'Of course I did! I'm not the villain you think me!'

'Don't fire up. I did not come here to fight you. We are older, perhaps wiser, and I would like to put the past behind us. I want to know my granddaughter.'

He walked across the room and sat down opposite her.

'She was born in a small village near Burton-on-Trent, called Burton under Needwood. If she had been given my name it's possible you might have traced me.'

'You appear to have changed your name too, Mr Eastwood.'

'For the same reason. Besides, my father's name was still remembered, even after a dozen years. I did not wish that scandal to touch my daughter. Even though you had rejected us, I hoped to give her the sort of advantages she would have had if you had forgiven Abigail.'

Lady Catherine sighed.

'How often I have wished we had behaved differently. I didn't hear of her death until some years afterwards, and we tried to trace you then. The person who told me knew she had borne a child, but not whether it was a boy or girl, or even if it lived. Did she die in childbirth?'

'Yes. She lost too much blood, and died in my arms twelve hours after Abby was born. She was weak, but not in great pain. Believe me, ma'am, I wished with all my heart I had not persisted in marrying her. If I had not, and not given her a child, she might be alive today.'

Lady Catherine reached across and placed her hand on his arm.

'How can we tell? She loved you, and I am sure was happy with you for the short time you had. She would not have been happy if she had married where we wished. And she could still have died. Childbirth is dangerous. Don't blame yourself. And you would not have had Abby.'

He nodded. 'I was fortunate to find a good woman in the village, who had lost twins, and she became Abby's nurse. She had other children, and would not leave them, so I had no option but to leave Abby with her for a while. When she was two years old I persuaded Emily Jordan to care for her. Emily's husband was an old schoolfriend, and they had no children. I saw her as often as I could go to Bath.'

'But she is unaware you are her father?'

'She knows me as her trustee. It seemed best, seeing the sort of life I led. I was determined to try and give her all possible advantages. Meanwhile, I had to earn money to provide for her, to ensure she had enough to take to a husband.'

'Julian Wantock does not appear to want money with her, if what I hear is correct.'

'He'll have it, all the same. I think what I can give her matches his own fortune.'

Lady Catherine raised her eyebrows, and he smiled.

'I have been fortunate, but it was all gained honestly. I had no desire to follow in my father's footsteps.'

'I assume he is dead?'

'I assume so too. He went to France in '86, after that duel, but I heard nothing apart from one letter saying he had settled in Paris.

261

If he did not die in the Revolution he was probably killed by another of the men he cheated.'

'Your life has not been easy. You have never remarried?'

'I have never been tempted after loving your daughter.'

'So, Mr Eastwood, what do we do now? It will be a great shock to Abby, so do I tell her, or will you?'

'She has to know?'

'It would be cruel, to all of us, to keep her in ignorance. Besides, she would be our heir. We have no one else, and there is no title to pass on, or entailed land. My parents considered I married beneath me,' she added, with a sigh, 'so I should have been more sympathetic to Abigail when she fell in love with you. But they did not disown me as we did Abigail.'

'Might the earl or his mother object, once they know my history?'

'I'll tell the countess myself. I knew her well at one time. Let me tell Abby too.'

Mr Wood breathed a deep sigh.

'I ought to do it, but I confess it could be better coming from you, my lady. When will you tell her?'

'I will ask her to visit me tomorrow. I am staying at the Pulteney, she can come to see me there. It will be more private than in Hill Street. By the way, why did you choose Lady Padmore to bring her out? I saw her earlier, and I am afraid I did not take to her.'

Mr Wood frowned, and threw up his hands.

'That was another error of judgement. She was suggested to me by a friend who knew she was hoping to bring out Caroline. She has a very low income, and jumped at the chance to earn a fee, and live in a good part of Town. I was so thankful, knowing her connection with the Wantocks, that I did not enquire deeply enough into her character.'

'It does not appear to have damaged Abby. She's a charming girl, and I shall be very happy to acknowledge her. She can be married from our house if she wishes, and you have no objections.'

★ ★ ★

Abby was puzzled, the following morning, to receive an invitation to visit Lady Catherine at the Pulteney Hotel. A maid would be sent to escort her if she was able to come, the note said. Lady Padmore, thoroughly reconciled to Caroline's betrothal, had taken her straight to her favourite modiste's to order a wedding gown, and Abby thought they would be shopping for as long as Lady Padmore could stand. She had no hesitation in sending back an acceptance, and an hour later was entering the hotel in Piccadilly and being shown to her ladyship's suite of rooms.

Lady Catherine was looking out of the window, and turned to beckon Abby to join her.

'This is the suite which the Tsar and his sister occupied when they came for the peace celebrations,' she said. 'Apparently the Regent was most offended, but I cannot say I blamed them. It would have been very difficult if they had stayed at Carlton House. This way they were able to avoid some of the Regent's more extravagant parties.'

'I would have liked to have seen something of them,' Abby said. 'We heard such a lot about them in Bath, and I think quite a few of the visitors came to drink the waters after the excesses.'

Lady Catherine laughed.

'I'm sure they did. Now, child, sit down, over here.'

She guided Abby to a sopha next to a small table, and Abby frowned when she saw smelling salts, a vinaigrette, some hartshorn, and a decanter of brandy on it.

'Ma'am, are you unwell?' she asked in some alarm. 'I ought not to be here if you are feeling ill. Is it faintness, like the other night?'

Lady Catherine laughed and took Abby's hand in hers.

'No, my dear. I don't expect to need it, but it is as well to be prepared. I'm afraid I am going to give you a shock.'

'Me? You think I might need something?' Abby asked, incredulous. She was not a girl given to the vapours. 'What sort of a shock?'

'The other night, my faintness was caused by seeing you. I thought my daughter had come back to life. You are so like her, my dear child.'

'Daughter? You mean — but it's impossible!'

'My daughter eloped with your father twenty years ago. You are my grandchild. There is no doubt about it. Apart from your looks.'

She picked up a miniature which had been lying face down on the table, and handed it to Abby. After a startled glance at her Abby looked at the painting and blinked in disbelief. The dress was old-fashioned, with a deep collar, but the face staring back at her could have been her own. The hair was a rich auburn, the eyes violet, and the very shape of her chin and nose and cheeks were depicted in the exquisite little portrait.

She looked up at Lady Catherine.

'I — I don't know what to say. You are her

mother? My grandmother?'

'Her name was Abigail too. She died when you were born, and your father placed you with Lady Jordan, in the mistaken belief he could not provide for you adequately.'

'My father? But how do you know this, my lady? He died when I was a baby too.'

'No, my dear, he didn't. I talked to him yesterday. You have always known him as Mr Wood, but his real name, as yours is, is Eastwood.'

'Mr Wood? He is my father, and he has never told me?'

Abby sprang to her feet and began to pace the room. She could not take it in, could not believe it. How could she suddenly discover that a man she had known all her life had kept her in ignorance of their relationship?

She swung round and faced Lady Catherine.

'Why? Why did he deceive me? And I suppose Barton isn't my name either? Or were they not married? But then my name would be Simon, I suppose.'

'They were married. He will tell you the reasons he changed your name, and his, but he thought it was for the best you were not known to be his daughter. You were born at a village called Barton, somewhere in Staffordshire, I believe.'

Abby sat down again, and put her face in her hands.

'I can't believe this.'

'Are you faint?' Lady Catherine asked anxiously. 'Here, take these smelling salts.'

Abby shook her head and waved them away.

'I must go to see him. I must know the truth.'

'He is at home; he will be expecting you. Would you like me to come with you?'

'No, thank you.'

'I'll send you in my carriage. Then I hope you will both come back here and dine with me. There is such a lot to say, so many years to catch up on.'

Abby nodded, but said nothing. She had not fully taken in the news, but she was growing more and more furious with Mr Wood. She could not think of him as her father. Not yet. She had to talk to him, soon.

15

Abby almost ran out of the hotel and turned along Piccadilly. She was shaking with fury and not attending to where she was going. As she crossed the road an exquisite driving a curricle had to swerve to avoid her, and a coach driver leaned down and swore vividly at stupid molls who had nothing better to do than try to kill themselves. She was oblivious.

It was not until she was walking down St James's Street, and a pair of fops closed in and accosted her that she noticed where she was. All she had been thinking about was the quickest way to reach the house where Mr Wood lived in St James's Square, and she had forgotten than no respectable lady was ever seen in the area of the clubs, open to insult from the men seated in the windows or dandies on the street.

She glared at them so ferociously they dropped back, and let her pass, but sent mocking jibes after her. She scarcely heard them. Her whole attention was on what she would say to Mr Wood — her father.

How could he leave her in total ignorance

of their kinship? How could he let her believe her father was dead? Why had he not permitted her to live with him? Why had he never told her anything but the bare facts about her mother and the elopement? Why had he changed his name and given her a false one?

By the time she reached his house and hammered on the door her head was bursting with questions, anger, and a deep misery she did not stop to analyse, and she could barely stammer out a request to see Mr Wood.

'You are Miss Barton?' the butler asked, and all Abby could do was nod her head.

'But it's not my name,' she whispered to herself, as the man opened the door wider and gestured to her to enter.

'Please come in, Miss Barton. Mr Wood is expecting you.'

She followed him blindly up a sweeping staircase. She had never been to the house before, and was only dimly conscious of her surroundings. On the first floor the butler knocked lightly on a door, and in response to some command from within opened it and stood back to permit Abby to enter. The moment she was inside he closed the door softly. The faint click brought Abby out of her stupor, and she took a deep breath and looked across at the man standing by one of the long windows.

'Abby, my dear. Her ladyship has told you?'

His air of calmness ignited Abby's anger to a new level, and she clenched her fists and took an impetuous step towards him.

'You are really my father?' she demanded, her voice quivering with passion. 'You have never told me, let me believe I had no one? Why? You are despicable, and I hate you, and never wish to see you ever again!'

He came towards her slowly.

'Abby, there were reasons. Let me explain, and I can only hope you will understand, even if you can never forgive me.'

'Oh, that's unlikely! I want to understand how anyone could be so unfeeling, so despicable!'

'Then come and sit down, my dear. Can I get you a glass of Madeira, or ratafia?'

'I want nothing from you, just an explanation. And I am not your *dear*, I don't think I ever was. I suppose I was an embarrassment to you,' she flung at him. 'Don't touch me!' she added as he tried to take her hand and guide her to a chair.

'Very well, but do sit down. My explanation may take some time.'

'It can take until doomsday, you will never convince me you were justified in denying me a family.'

She sat down and he took a chair opposite her.

'Bear with me, Abby. I know this is difficult for you, but recounting my background is not easy for me. Try to understand.'

★ ★ ★

Julian was just entering the house when a carriage drew up in the square, and he glanced over his shoulder to see Lady Catherine descending. He hastened across to help her.

She smiled at him, but he discerned worry in her face.

'My dear boy,' she said, and he almost laughed. 'I came to warn you. Abby has been given some rather shocking news, and she will need your understanding. She has gone to see Mr Wood, and I cannot hazard a guess about her response.'

'Will you come inside and explain?'

'If I may.'

When she was installed in his library, sipping at some ratafia, he sat opposite her and waited. She took a deep sigh.

'Abby is my granddaughter,' she began abruptly. 'I saw her at the Quinton ball and she is the image of her mother. That is not greatly disturbing her, though, of course, it was a shock. More of a shock was discovering that instead of being dead, as she has always been told, her father is very much alive. It is Mr Wood. She has gone to confront him, and I imagine that will be an explosive encounter. She has plenty of spirit, like my own Abigail.'

'And he never told her?' Julian asked, and tried to clamp down on his emotions of anger and disgust at a man who could treat his own daughter in such a fashion.

'No. He had his reasons, some of which may have been good ones. It is not for me to judge. But I cannot give away all his secrets, he must tell you those himself. I came to ask you to understand Abby. She will need your support.'

'Of course she has it, totally.'

'I thought you would say that. I intend to invite her to visit me at Compton, and if she wishes, she may be married from there. But be patient with her. It has been an enormous shock.'

Julian, uncharacteristically, felt he needed advice. How would Abby feel? Did she need solitude to think about this, or would it help her to be able to talk to him?

'Should I go and fetch her from Mr Wood's house? Is that where she has gone?'

'Yes. He will see her safely back to Hill Street, don't fear. I cannot tell what she will want to do, but one thing I'm sure she will not do is confide in Lady Padmore.'

'Indeed not. I will go there later and try to see her. If she refuses me I will leave a note asking her to send for me when she is ready to talk. You will not be leaving London yet?'

'Not for a few days, and I hope when I do I will be taking Abby home with me. You will be very welcome to join us.'

'If she wants me, I will do so with pleasure. Thank you for coming to warn me.'

He saw her back to her carriage, and then went back to his library, to pace up and down as he tried to imagine what could cause a man to deny his daughter, and the feelings of that daughter once she discovered the truth.

★ ★ ★

'I have to start with my family,' Mr Wood said slowly. He had been preparing for this meeting ever since Abby's betrothal, knowing he would need to be open with her and the earl, but he still found it difficult.

'And mine,' Abby said, her voice cold.

'And yours. I have tried to forget it for thirty years, but it is the reason — one of them — for my deception. Eighty years ago my grandfather, Jack Westwood, was hanged at Tyburn. He had been a highwayman for several years.'

'Tyburn?'

Her shock and horror were obvious. He wished he could spare her this, but she had a right to know.

'He deserved it. He'd stolen and frightened people for many years.'

'Westwood? Not Eastwood? Then what is my real name? I am bewildered.'

At least she was listening to him.

'Your name is what you prefer to be called.'

'You haven't forgotten, or you would not have called your club the East and West.'

'Perhaps you are right, my dear. Perhaps I intended it as a rather sick joke only I could appreciate. I benefited from the money he stole, but it was what I had earned honestly that financed the club. I don't have it on my conscience that stolen money set me up for my future successes.'

'What else is there?'

'It gets worse. My father, who was called John Eastwood, lived by gambling. Worse, he cheated his dupes. And in '86 he killed one of them in a duel. The man had accused him, almost certainly correctly, of fudging the cards. He fled to France because the man's brothers were threatening vengeance.'

'Is he still there?'

'I don't know. But he would be in his seventies by now, so he is most likely dead, even if he managed to stay away from vengeful men he had robbed. He sent me one letter from Paris, but I have heard no more. I have no doubt he changed his name again, so even if I wanted to find him I could not. And I most certainly have no desire ever to see him again.'

'We have both been unfortunate in our fathers,' Abby murmured, and he winced.

'I am sorry for that. But enough about my parent.'

'What of your mother? And grandmother?'

'My grandmother died when my father was born, or so I have been told. I don't think I shall be suddenly confronted with her as you were with Lady Simon.'

'And your mother?'

'She lived for ten years after he left England and deserted her. I was sixteen and at Eton when the duel happened. It was his dishonest money that paid for me to be there, and where I learned some of the attributes of a gentleman, which enabled me to pursue my future career. But there was not any left for me to go to Oxford, as I had intended.'

He detected a slight softening of her attitude.

'Your mother. She was deserted. Had she

anyone to help her?'

'Myself only. I was sixteen, but I looked older. I had wasted some of my youth learning to play cards. My father taught me all the tricks he used. I had to support my mother somehow, so I turned to gambling. I never, I promise you, cheated directly. But I knew I was more skilled than most, even at that age. I never played games of pure chance, only those where skill might win.'

'Could you not have entered some more genteel occupation?'

'I was too old to become an apprentice, and did not have the right contacts, besides being too young, for what you call genteel occupations. I did not, then, have, or see how I could acquire, sufficient capital to open a business which would have provided us with more than a bare living. I did not even have any to open a small shop, and frankly, I did not fancy life as an itinerant pedlar. So I turned to gambling, trusting in my skill and luck to support us.'

'And you were only sixteen. How did you do it?'

The hostility was lessening, and he knew she was becoming interested in the story. He breathed a sigh of relief.

'I was of an age to mix with the wealthy undergraduates at Oxford and Cambridge.

Indeed, many of them were my former schoolfriends. Through them I obtained introductions to other rich men. I even attended some lectures,' he added reminiscently. 'I've always regretted not being able to take a degree.'

'But the gambling?'

'I was desperate. My mother was in lodgings in Islington, had no money to pay the rent which was overdue. She could have been turned out, penniless, within days. I walked to Oxford, and within a week had won sufficient to pay her debts and leave her enough for the following month. Then I walked to Cambridge and my luck held. After this I was able to travel on the stage. I moved around, to provincial cities where I might find bored, wealthy young men. Places like Manchester and Birmingham, Bristol and Leeds. I went back to Oxford and Cambridge occasionally, until I was too old to pass as an undergraduate or one of their friends. I spent time at watering places, in Brighton, but never too long in one place. As well as supporting my mother I saved, for one day I had plans to set up a club. Then she died.'

'I'm sorry.'

'I think she was glad to go. My father's desertion had broken her heart, for despite his being a rogue and a cheat she loved him.

But it freed me; I could travel more widely without having to go back to London. I went to the Baltic ports, to rich trading cities like Amsterdam, and some of the German spa towns, even occasionally to France when I could get there. Then two years later I met your mother in Bath.'

'Bath?'

'I think it was sentiment that had me place you there. Lord Jordan was an old friend from school; that is how I knew Lady Jordan.'

'What happened? You and Mama?'

'Her parents disliked me. Lady Catherine then was very conscious of her own importance as the daughter of an Irish duke. Her husband was not titled, but came from a very old family which had, I understand, often refused titles in the past. They took her back home to Gloucestershire. But I knew the son of a neighbour, and he was sympathetic. The Simons wished Abigail to marry him, as it would unite the two estates, but he was in love with someone else, so he was prepared to help me. I stayed there for a month, and contrived meetings with your mother. Her parents were implacable, they discovered these meetings, and threatened to have me sent to prison or transported. They could have done so; it would be easy for them to charge me, and they would have been believed.'

'But that's monstrous! And Lady Catherine appears such a sweet old lady now.'

'Indeed. She has changed,' he said with a wry smile.

'So you eloped?'

'We could see no alternative. We set off for Gretna, were married, and for a while we travelled round Scotland. I continued playing with any young fool I met, to support us. But I never ruined anyone, Abby. I always called a halt before they could hazard their last guineas, or their horses. I was making enough to live on comfortably and still save. Then you were expected and Abigail wished to be closer to her home. I think she hoped her parents would forgive us when we gave them a grandchild. But it wasn't to be.'

He paused, and Abby rose from her chair to come and kneel beside him. He took her hand and held it to his cheek.

'You loved her very much, did you not?' she asked softly.

He nodded, took a deep breath, and continued.

'We travelled south by easy stages. I was still playing, in the mill towns and the spas. We were last at Matlock and Buxton, and were planning to go to Cheltenham, where we hoped we might hear news of her family, and discover what their attitude towards us might be. But we left it too late. We were staying at the little village of Barton under Needwood, just south of Burton-on-Trent, when her pains began.'

'And she died?'

'In my arms. I was devastated, blamed myself, and swore I would give you as good a life as she had had as a girl. I had to leave you with a wet nurse, but then Emily Jordan took you. She did not know I was your father; she thought I was a friend, so don't blame her for keeping my secret.'

'Why make it a secret? That is the thing I cannot understand.'

'I may have been wrong, but I thought the daughter of a man who lived by gambling would not be accepted in Society.'

'Many of the *ton* lose fortunes gambling.'

'But that is inherited money, usually, not what they have themselves acquired by gambling or business. It is respectable. I was not.'

'It's a foolish distinction.'

'But it is there, the prejudice. I wanted you to have what you would have had if your mother had married as her parents wished. So I felt I had to keep our relationship a secret. I soon made profits from the club. I worked hard to make it a place men could relax in, as well as gamble. I began other ventures with the profits; they were successful and my fortune doubled and trebled. Now most of my business is in the City, respectable if only trade. My early money was not respectable, and I wanted you to have the best opportunity possible for a good marriage.'

'I see.'

Abby had taken his revelations remarkably well, he decided, and was thankful.

'Does Julian know this?' she asked.

'I will tell him later today. Now, my cook had prepared a nuncheon for us. Let us go down and eat, and if you have any more questions I can answer them for you.'

'I have dozens, and I want to know all about my mother.'

★   ★   ★

Julian came to her later that day, in his phaeton, and took her driving in the Park. They barely spoke until they were through the gates, then Abby glanced nervously at him.

'You know?' she asked.

'Yes. Your father was with me earlier. He told me all, my love. It must have been a great shock to you.'

Abby was trying to be cheerful, but her mood swung between a certain pleasure in discovering she had a family after all, and a residual anger that she had been kept in ignorance all this time.

'It's been a shock for you too. You are not getting the bride you thought I was.'

'You are the same, the Abby I love. The Abby I mean to marry. Lady Catherine sent a message hoping we would call on her tomorrow morning, at her hotel.'

'Yes, she sent me one too. She has asked me to go to stay with her. Julian, I don't know what to do!'

He could not prevent himself from laughing.

'I think that is the first time I have known you have any doubts at all,' he said. 'Usually my Abby knows exactly what to do in all circumstances.'

She smiled at that, but was still subdued.

'Does Lady Padmore know?'

'I told her about Mr Wood being my father, but she does not know the whole. She has asked endless questions, but fortunately she is preoccupied with buying Caroline's bride clothes. Does your mother know?'

'Yes, I asked Mr Wood to tell her while I came to you. I felt it would be better for her to be able to hear it directly from him.'

Abby felt a twinge of compassion for her father, This would be the third time, the fourth if he had told Lady Catherine, he had been forced to recount the details of his reasons for not acknowledging her. She had no doubt that soon the entire *ton* would, in that mysterious way gossip spreads, know all the details. It would be odious for her to face the sniggering looks, the sly innuendoes, even the cuts from the high sticklers, but she was about to escape, and need never come to London again. He would be forced to remain here, at the mercy of all those who would despise him.

Julian soon took her back, saying he would call for her the following morning to escort her to the Pulteney. She went up to her room and sat by the window, thinking over all she had learned, until it was time for dinner.

They had no engagements for once, and Abby was hoping she could escape to bed early. She was exhausted from all the emotion. Dudley was out, to her relief, and Caroline and Lady Padmore deep in animated discussion of what was necessary for her trousseau. They all three looked up in surprise when a visitor was announced.

It was Lady Jane Ilroy. She swept into the drawing room and gave Abby a brief nod before crossing to kiss Lady Padmore.

'You poor dear,' she cried. 'I am so devastated to think of my own cousin having to endure such terrible things. First this alliance with trade, and now, even worse, you have been tricked into giving your countenance to the daughter of a card sharp, the descendant of a murderer, and a highwayman.'

Abby fired up at once. How had the woman learned all these details?

'My father has never cheated at cards! And how do you know about him?'

'I was with my mother when he came to confess. I suppose he felt it better to tell us his version before we heard from others. That's what he says, but what proof have you?' she sneered. 'Whatever he protests about his innocence people will always suspect. After all, he encouraged a young, innocent girl to elope, and from what he told Mama dragged her all over the country while he fleeced whoever he could trick into playing with him.'

'That's not true!' Abby protested.

'It's charming of you to say you believe him,' Lady Jane said, 'but if you have any honour in you, you will give up Julian. He will be smirched by the connection if this ridiculous engagement goes ahead. If you love him do you really want that to happen? To have him shunned by his former friends? Having no one of importance inviting him anywhere? Because they will not wish to have to invite you too. He would not be able to take a position in the Ministry, something his birth entitles him too and for which he is admirably suited, and would enjoy. Oh, my dear, I know you're innocent, and did not even know the wretch was your father, but that makes it worse. People will ask what was really behind his secrecy.'

Even more furious at her pretended solicitude than at her sneers, Abby abruptly excused herself and went to bed. She did not care if it was rude. If she stayed she would be even ruder and tell Lady Jane just what she thought of her.

During a sleepless night, however, Abby began to wonder if Lady Jane was right. She knew the *ton* intimately. She would know what people would think and say. By dawn she had come to accept that if she married Julian she would be harming him. He had made it plain he still wished to marry her, but that was his innate chivalry and sense of honour. Having once offered and been accepted, he could not withdraw. But she could.

As soon as it was light she rose from her bed, packed a few things in a small valise, and wrote two notes. The one for her maid was easy, but the other cost her many anguished pangs. By the time it was finished it was blotched with tears, but she dared not take the time to copy it. Taking the valise, donning her travelling cloak, and making sure her purse, with all the money she had about her, was safely in the pocket, she crept down the back stairs and through the kitchens to the stables. Rusty jumped up from where he lay on a pile of straw and licked her face. She tied on his collar, hushed him, and led him out.

She had to take the note to Grosvenor Square herself, to make sure Julian received it, but she found an urchin who took it to the door in exchange for sixpence. As soon as she saw it safely delivered she found a hansom cab and asked to be taken to Chelsea.

The cabbie objected, first to Rusty's presence in the cab, then in doubt Abby could pay the fare. Terrified that any delay might lead to her capture, she agreed to pay him in advance, and they set off. She breathed a sigh of relief. Now all that was left to her was a return to Bath and a slow decline into aged spinsterhood.

16

'Abby, don't be silly!'

'I thought you'd support me,' Abby said, swallowing hard. 'Aunt Emily, I can't marry him now! It wouldn't be fair! His sister was right, any connection with me would be a disaster for him. Please, can we not go to Bath? If we start soon we can be in Marlborough tonight.'

Lady Jordan shook her head. She had been roused early from her bed and was still in her wrapper. She poured Abby another cup of tea.

'Be reasonable, Abby. I cannot pack and leave in so short a time. Besides, Mrs Hughes deserves more consideration. She has been such a friend to me, and a wonderful hostess. It would be most impolite to leave her so abruptly.'

'But he'll find me! He'll know this is the only place I can go to.'

'If he follows you, does that not prove his love for you?'

'All it would prove is his sense of honour, in not abandoning me. But I can free him. If you won't take me back home I'll hire my own chaise.'

'Where is Ellie? Why did you not bring her here?'

'I left her a note and some money, telling her to come on the stage, and bring the rest of my clothes.'

'I can't believe how foolish you are being, child. If you are determined to go, why not take your maid with you, and all your belongings?'

'I couldn't stay in Hill Street any longer, for fear Julian came and prevented me. And he will follow me here as soon as he receives my note, I know he will, so I have to leave quickly.'

'Are you expecting him to drag you back by force? Why can you not be sensible and discuss it with him?'

'Do you think this is easy for me? I think I loved him from the moment I first saw him, and it was like a dream come true when he loved me too. But that was before I knew about my father, and how he has lived by gambling. Oh, he says he never cheated anyone, and I do believe him, but it is still not a respectable occupation.'

'It is a business, not so different from Hartley's, and Lady Padmore has accepted him.'

'Because of his money. That is all she cares about. But I have not told you all, yet, just about Mr Wood concealing from me the fact he is my father, which is hurtful enough, but I did understand his motives. He told me a good deal more, but his father killed a man in a duel as well as being a card sharp, who lived by cheating, and fled to France, where nothing more was heard of him. Why, he might still be alive!'

'It seems unlikely as he must be quite old now, and France has been in turmoil for years. But a man cannot help his father.'

'People will say there is bad blood. There might be. Who knows if there is any truth in it, and if Julian and I had children, it might come out in them!' She shuddered, 'Besides, there is more. His father, my great-grandfather, was a highwaymen and was hanged at Tyburn.'

'Oh, my dear, you have had so many shocks your mind is disordered, and you cannot make decisions in that state. Did you sleep at all last night?'

Abby reluctantly had to admit she had not. 'I can sleep in the coach,' she insisted.

'Please, my dear, don't be so hasty. Wait and see what the earl does. If he accepts your refusal then we will return to Bath. If he does not, we can discuss it calmly. Now, I intend to treat you like a baby, give you a tisane to help you sleep, and put you to bed for a few hours.

I am sure, when you have rested, you will be able to make a proper decision.'

Abby protested, but she was suddenly exhausted, and the thought of a soft goose down mattress was tempting. Aunt Emily had been like a mother to her, always kind, but firm when necessary, and Abby respected her as fair and wise. The prospect of finding a post chaise, and setting off on a long journey alone, for she knew Lady Jordan would refuse to accompany her today, was suddenly too daunting.

'Very well,' she sighed, and was led up to one of Mrs Hughes's spare rooms. Within minutes of discarding her gown and shoes she was asleep.

★   ★   ★

Julian was being shaved when his valet brought in a note for him.

'It was delivered earlier this morning, your lordship.'

'Thank you, put it there. I will read it when I am dressed and ready to go out.'

It was ten minutes later before he had donned the plush breeches with strings and rosettes to each knee, the blue waistcoat with its inch-wide yellow stripes and the spotted neckerchief. He shrugged on the long driving coat with its large mother of pearl buttons, and only remembered the note as his valet handed him the deep-crowned hat.

He broke the wafer sealing it and scanned it quickly, then with an oath strode to the door.

'My curricle, send for it, at once.'

'My lord, the barouche is at the door, waiting.'

'Then that will have to do.'

He ran down the stairs and leaped into the yellow-bodied barouche. Unlike most members of the Four-Horse Club his team were not bays, but blacks. He had once jokingly told the other members that the silver-mounted harness looked better on their silky coats. Within seconds the team, more used to a sedate trot than a faster pace, were being urged into a canter towards Hill Street, instead of the usual route towards Cavendish Square.

He drew to a halt outside Lady Padmore's house, and pounded on the door. When the butler opened it he stepped inside.

'Miss Barton, where is she?' he demanded. 'Is she here?'

'I understand Miss Barton left at some very early hour,' the man replied.

'Was she alone?'

'I believe so, my lord. Her maid is here,

taking on somewhat awful,' he confided, descending from lofty heights.

Julian thought rapidly. 'Did she take the dog?'

'I have not heard.'

'Then be a good fellow and send to the stables while I talk to Lady Padmore. Is she upstairs?'

'Yes my lord, with — '

He stopped, for the earl had bounded up the stairs three at a time. Shrugging, he decided to lower his dignity by going to the stables himself. The man was clearly in a vast hurry, and it would be quicker to take the message himself, and receive any token of thanks the earl would be sure to bestow.

Julian halted on the threshold of the drawing room. Caroline was huddled in a chair and had clearly been weeping. Her mother sat stiffly upright, but to Julian's fury his sister Jane was also present.

'Where is Abby?' he demanded.

'I wash my hands of the wretched girl,' Lady Padmore cried. 'I have no idea where the ungrateful chit has gone. After all I have done for her she steals out in the dead of night and vanishes.'

'Good riddance,' Lady Jane said. 'I trust, Julian, that after this display of hoydenism you will see sense and repudiate her. There are far better and more suitable matches for you than the granddaughter of a murderer! Caroline here would make a far better countess.'

'Caroline is betrothed,' he began angrily, but Lady Padmore interrupted.

'It is not certain, Cousin.'

'Not certain? Have you lost all sense of propriety? Pray furnish me with the address where Lady Jordan is staying. It is in Chelsea, I believe?'

'Don't tell him,' Lady Jane said sharply. 'We don't want him to fetch the little wretch back.'

'I have no intention of telling him,' Lady Padmore said, but her voice was unsteady.

'It's in Sloane Street,' Caroline said, looking defiantly at her mother.

With a brief smile at her Julian turned and ran back down the stairs. The butler, puffing, was just coming from the back of the house.

'The dog is gone, my lord, very early, long before any of the grooms were about.'

'Thank you.' The earl flung him a coin, and not waiting for him to open the door, was outside and in the barouche before the butler reached the front door.

*   *   *

It was just after noon when Abby was woken by a pounding on the front door. She felt rested after her doze, and wondered for a few moments who was in such a hurry to be admitted. Then she gasped. Could it be the earl? She stole to the window and looked out, and breathed a sigh of relief. If he had come he would have been driving his phaeton or curricle, not that garish yellow barouche that stood, with a steaming team of horses, outside the house.

She had not had time to consider what to do. Perhaps she could stay here and persuade Lady Jordan to go to Bath tomorrow. She might even send for Ellie and the rest of her possessions. She had left in a panic, she now admitted, and it would be more sensible for them to travel together.

She put on her gown and was brushing her hair when Lady Jordan entered the room.

'My dear, the earl is here and wishes to speak with you.'

'Julian? Oh, no! I can't! Please deny me, Aunt Emily, I don't want to see him.'

'But I wish to see you, my love, and I am not going to be denied.'

Julian entered the room and stood there watching her with an unreadable expression in his eyes.

Abby began to quake. He looked odd in

that deplorable blue and yellow waistcoat, and the spotted neckerchief, so unlike his normal elegant clothes. And he sounded implacable.

'You owe me an explanation for this ridiculous piece of fiction,' he added, waving the note she had sent him.

'I don't want to talk. I am determined, I have made up my mind and I cannot marry you.'

He grinned. 'I am determined too, and I am going to marry you. I think we will go for a drive in my barouche. Everyone will stare to see a female in one of the Four-Horse Club carriages, no doubt, but we will avoid their route. We'll take a gentle drive to Richmond Park while we talk.'

'No. I won't come.'

'You will come willingly or I will carry you down and throw you in the carriage. Which do you prefer, my love?'

Abby cast a hunted glance at Lady Jordan and surprised a smile on her face. So there would be no help there. She sighed.

'You could no doubt do that, but it would only strengthen my determination. Very well, my lord, I will come for a drive with you. Am I permitted to put on my pelisse?'

He bowed, and when she had slipped into the pelisse and fixed her bonnet, he offered her his arm and led her down the stairs.

Abby fumed inwardly, but permitted him to help her on to the box seat of the barouche. Despite herself she felt a thrill at the notion of sitting behind a team of horses, like a coachman.

Julian climbed up beside her.

'It would be impossible to talk if you sat in the back, so I trust you do not object?'

'No. Why are you wearing these odd clothes? And why did you not come in your curricle?' she asked. Making polite but cool conversation would, she decided, show him she did not intend to change her mind.

'These odd clothes, my love, are the uniform of the Four-Horse Club. So is the barouche. I was about to drive out with them when your note was brought to me. I deemed it better to use the vehicle available rather than wait for another to be harnessed. I was afraid you might have left already.'

'I've heard of that club. What do you do?'

'Nothing exciting, I promise you. We meet in Cavendish Square and drive in procession to Salt Hill where we have dinner. We never drive above a trot. We stay the night at Turnham Green.'

'That sounds tedious,' Abby said.

'But it is a great honour to be asked to join. It is only for the most accomplished whipsters. My team, though, are accustomed to a sedate pace, and were rather dismayed to be asked for more, so I will not push them now.'

They drove in silence for a while. Abby could think of nothing else to say, and Julian did not appear to be in a hurry to talk. Then when there were fewer houses he suddenly spoke.

'What makes you think you are not fit to marry me, as you said in your note?'

'It will hurt you,' she replied. 'If you are connected to me, people will despise you. I am not respectable.'

'That is a slur on Lady Jordan.'

'Aunt Emily? Why should it be?'

'If you are not respectable, they may consider she is not either. After all, she brought you up and presumably taught you how to go on in respectable society.'

'That's ridiculous! But my father is a gambler, and his father was even worse, for he cheated.'

'And killed his man in a duel.'

'Yes, and his father was hanged; he was a highwayman!'

'Many girls would consider a highwayman ancestor romantic.'

'I am not many girls!'

He laughed. 'No, you are my own darling love.'

Abby blinked hard. Why did he make it so hard for her to maintain her refusal?

'They were disreputable! I'm ashamed of them!'

'Perhaps we all have ancestors we could be ashamed of, if we bothered. One of mine was a pirate.'

'A pirate? One of the Keighleys?'

'Yes. He sailed with Prince Rupert.'

'Surely that was not real piracy? Isn't it privateering, something that was allowed?'

'I doubt the seamen they fought cared for the difference. Another was one of the men who turned nuns out of their convents. One went on crusade and boasted about how many Saracens he had killed in an ambush, women and children as well as men.'

'Oh, no!' Abby stared at him in consternation.

'So you see my family have embarrassing ancestors too. Even further back one was a Viking who raped and pillaged when they invaded. Another was a caveman who specialized in dragging his women — he had many — into a cave by their hair.'

Abby was betrayed into a giggle.

'You can't know that! You are making it up!'

'It could have happened. I am trying to show you, my darling, that none of us can claim absolute purity in our families. So your arguments are false, and you are going to marry me.'

'I'm not,' she said, but her voice was uncertain. 'You can't want me,' she said in some desperation.

He pulled the horses to a halt and turned to her.

'If I did not want you more than I have ever wanted anything in my life before, we wouldn't be here. Abby, I don't know if you would be miserable if we parted. I suspect so, as it is misguided chivalry that makes you try to deny me, not lack of love. I know I would never be happy again. I could never marry anyone else. The title might even devolve on to Dudley,' he added. 'Wouldn't that please his mama? I don't think she had thought it through when she was trying to get me married to Caroline.'

Abby was struggling with genealogical lines. 'But surely Dudley is not a Keighley, so how could he inherit?'

'He can't, but it might be someone as dreadful. Won't you save us from that, my love?'

'I — I can't. Oh Julian, how can I?'

'Very easily, my silly sweet darling. We forget this and go back to prepare for our wedding. Oh, come here,' he said, and drew her towards him.

He pushed her bonnet away, cupped her head in his hand, and bent his face towards hers. His lips met hers just as a stage-coach overtook them, and Abby heard whistles and laughter from the passengers seated on the roof. She didn't care. He loved her, and had made light of her fears. Together they could face anyone. She kissed him back enthusiastically. It was some time before he turned the barouche and took her back to Sloane Street.

★ ★ ★

Lady Catherine persuaded Abby and Lady Jordan to accompany her back to Compton. Mr Wood, it transpired, owned a small estate nearby and would be travelling there as soon as he could arrange business matters.

'I bought it out of sentiment,' he told Abby. 'I felt I could be close to where I first met your mother.'

Julian also had business to settle, but he and his mother would join them at Compton shortly.

'Two unexpected visitors will surprise your grandfather,' Lady Catherine chuckled. 'I must prepare him for another influx.'

'Will he . . . welcome me?' Abby asked diffidently.

She was happy and secure in Lady

Catherine's affection, but would her mother's father, who had been defied and who must have been hurt that his authority had been challenged, welcome her as warmly? And would he accept her father?

'He will be delighted to have found you. He is old, my dear, many years older than I, and frail. He may not live much longer, but I hope he will live to see your first child. We had just the one, and it was a sorrow for him. He would have liked sons, and a large family.'

'And my father? He must have been so angry, hated him.'

'We were both very hurt, and implacable. For years we could not forgive, and did not reply to your mother's letters when she begged forgiveness. She stopped writing, and much later we heard she had died. Then, of course, we regretted our intransigence. But we could not change the past. At least in welcoming you and your father we can feel all is forgiven.'

Abby had forgiven him for his deceit, told him she fully understood his reasons, and said she had always felt a strong affection for him. That must have been family feeling. But would Mr Simon feel the same?

'I shall retain the name Wood,' her father had told her. 'I am well known by it and there would be confusion if I changed now.'

'But what am I to be called? I have such a choice!'

'You will soon be Lady Wantock, so it will no longer be a problem.'

After much thought Abby had decided she would be married from Compton, not her father's estate.

'Do you understand?' she asked anxiously. 'I feel it will make up, in some way, for my mother not being married from there.'

'The house is far larger than mine, and they will wish to invite many guests. It makes sense.' He looked disappointed, but soon rallied. 'I shall expect you and Julian to come and stay with me for a long visit when you return from your wedding journey.'

'Of course we will, and we'll come as often as you invite us.'

* * *

It was a glorious day late in July when Abby and Julian were married. Her favourite modiste from Bath had been summoned to Compton to make her wedding gown and several more gowns. Julian was taking his bride to Paris, first of all, and was too impatient to suffer a long delay while a trousseau was bought.

'You can purchase all those fripperies there,' he said.

Caroline and Anne were to be her bridesmaids. Caroline and Lady Padmore, the latter so effusive in her admiration of all things at Compton that Caroline confided she felt embarrassed by her, arrived two days before the ceremony. Anne and her parents were also staying.

Mr Simon, after the first shock, had welcomed Abby with tears in his faded eyes. They spent long hours together, he sitting in a chair in the drawing room or garden, and Abby curled up at his feet, stroking his hands. He recounted many stories of her mother's youth, and wished to know all about her own life in Bath.

Later Abby could recall only the look in Julian's eyes as her father led her down the aisle. Her gown of primrose silk was simply embroidered with gold thread. She wore no jewellery apart from her betrothal ring, and shivered as Julian placed the heavy gold band on her finger.

Afterwards the guests feasted at Compton. Lady Jane had refused to come, as had Dudley, but no one felt their absence did anything but improve the situation. Lady Catherine had supervised the guest list, and as well as Julian's friends, she had invited several of her daughter's old friends. Abby knew she would never recall their names, but she revelled in their compliments about her mother.

She was moving away from a conversation with two of these ladies when Julian appeared at her side.

'Come, it is time to go,' he said.

They left with good wishes, and some ribald comments from Julian's friends, ringing in their ears. He was driving his curricle, Ellie and his valet following in a chaise with all their luggage. Abby thought they were heading for Cheltenham, and looked at him in surprise when he turned off that road.

He grinned at her.

'Your father has lent us his house for two days. He has given all the servants leave of absence, and we will be totally alone. Ellie and Clark have gone on to Cheltenham. I shall be your maid.'

Abby blushed. 'Am I to be your valet? I don't promise to shave you without cutting you.'

'I can shave myself, but somehow I think that will be the last thing on my mind. I understand the servants have left us food, and I learned to brew tea and coffee and heat soup when I was in the army.'

'Somehow I don't think food will be much on our minds,' Abby murmured, and he glanced at her, then pulled the curricle to a halt and kissed her very thoroughly.

Breathless, she emerged from the embrace to see a couple of milkmaids looking at them and giggling. Julian tossed them some coins and asked them to wish him well, for he was just married, and the happiest man in England.

They arrived at the house, a charming little manor house built in the time of Queen Anne, to find a small pony harnessed to a gig outside the front door. As they drove towards it the door opened, and a manservant emerged.

'My lord, my lady, welcome. All is in readiness. I shall be at the main gatehouse lodge if you should require anything else.'

Before they had time to respond he clambered into the gig and gave the pony the office to move. Abby breathed a sigh of relief, suddenly shy. She discovered she did not wish anyone else to be near her while she and Julian spent the first few days of married life together.

Inside the house enticing smells came from a room to the right, and they found roasted chickens and beef set out on a table laid for two. A bottle of wine was open, and on the sideboard were cheeses and jellies and a bowl of strawberries with a jug of cream.

'I — need to brush my hair,' Abby said nervously. 'It has been blown into a tangle by the wind. Let us find the bedrooms first.'

Upstairs one door was open, to a large room where the bedcovers had been turned back. Abby went across to the bed and bounced on the soft feather mattress.

'Oh, this is comfortable. I can sleep here.'

'You will not be doing much sleeping,' Julian said, coming to sit beside her. 'Let me brush your hair.'

A brush lay on the toilet table, and he began to smooth her hair with long, slow strokes. Somehow, Abby did not know how, the fastenings of her bodice were loosened, and it fell down around her waist, with her arms trapped by the sleeves. She turned towards Julian, and he pulled her to him and kissed her.

All thought of food vanished as they fell back together on to the bed. Julian proved an excellent maid, she told him, and laughed when he refused to allow her to divest him of his clothes.

She had never before seen a naked man, and had not expected to find him beautiful. He was handsome, but that was different. His figure was strong and well-formed, his muscles rippling. When he came to her she buried her face in his chest in momentary shyness, but he gentled her as he would a nervous horse, stroking her and murmuring endearments, so that she forgot all except the incredible sensations he was rousing in her.

Long before he entered her she was panting for release from the tension building up inside her, and when it finally came she clung to him and wished never to let go.

'Abby, my sweetest love,' he murmured as they finally parted.

'Is that what marriage is?' she asked. 'If I'd known I'd have got married much earlier.'

'That is marriage. So are cold meats and all that awaits us downstairs. We had better eat after all that exercise.'

She laughed and sat up, unconcerned at her nakedness.

'Very well, my lord. But may we come back afterwards? I like being married to you.'

We do hope that you have enjoyed reading this large print book.

Did you know that all of our titles are available for purchase?

We publish a wide range of high quality large print books including:
Romances, Mysteries, Classics
General Fiction
Non Fiction and Westerns

Special interest titles available in large print are:
The Little Oxford Dictionary
Music Book
Song Book
Hymn Book
Service Book

Also available from us courtesy of Oxford University Press:
Young Readers' Dictionary
(large print edition)
Young Readers' Thesaurus
(large print edition)

For further information or a free brochure, please contact us at:
Ulverscroft Large Print Books Ltd.,
The Green, Bradgate Road, Anstey,
Leicester, LE7 7FU, England.
Tel: (00 44) **0116 236 4325**
Fax: (00 44) **0116 234 0205**

Other titles published by
The House of Ulverscroft:

SCANDAL AT THE DOWER HOUSE

Marina Oliver

When Catarina's elderly husband dies, she moves to the Dower House where things are about to change dramatically with the arrival of Catarina's young sister Joanna. Tricked by her cousin Matthew into a sham marriage, Joanna is now pregnant and alone. Catarina has a plan to hide her sister's disgrace, but then tragedy strikes suddenly at the Dower House. What will be the fate of Joanna's unwanted child?

SUPERVISING SALLY

Marina Oliver

Phoebe is delighted to go to Brussels as companion to Sally, rather than be an unpaid governess to her sister Jane's children. Her hopes are dashed when Zachary, Earl of Wrekin, claims Phoebe is too young for the task, and refuses to escort her. She finds herself unable to control the rebellious Sally, who gets into many scrapes even before they leave London. However, when Phoebe rescues Sally from a calamitous action, Zachary relents. But Jane's husband and his unpleasant sisters cause irritation on the journey. Then Napoleon escapes from Elba and everything is in turmoil for Phoebe.

A DISGRACEFUL AFFAIR

Marina Oliver

Sylvie Delamare's great-uncle Sir George sends her a mere £20 — claiming it to be a whole half of her inheritance — and she's infuriated. Her parents had been wealthy, so she wants to go and confront him in Norfolk. Meanwhile, she is invited to visit Lady Carstairs, her friend's aunt in London, to be presented. However, Sir Randal is suspicious of Sylvie, after seeing her with Monsieur Dupont, who he suspects is one of Napoleon's spies. Then when Sir Randal follows Dupont, he meets Sylvie in Norwich on her way to see Sir George. And when he offers her a lift — he becomes embroiled in her affairs . . .

THE ACCIDENTAL MARRIAGE

Marina Oliver

Julia goes with her sister Fanny and her husband Sir Frederick to Vienna, as governess to their daughters. There, the congress that is to settle the fate of Europe after the Napoleonic wars is gathering. Julia meets Sir Carey Evelegh, who has left his fiancée, Angelica, behind in England, with plans to return for a spring wedding. When Fanny sets off for home, Julia and her maid follow in another coach. But an accident on the way causes Julia to lose all her belongings. Now penniless, and a long way from home, who will help her to resolve her problem?

A MOST REBELLIOUS DEBUTANTE

Karen Abbott

Caught in the embrace of her dancing master, seventeen-year-old Lucy Templeton is banished to Montcliffe Hall. Here, she encounters the notorious Lord Rockhaven and a stolen kiss awakens something deep within her. Reluctantly, Lucy returns home and has a successful Season . . . but remembering that kiss, she refuses every offer of marriage. Then her former dancing master attempts to abduct her, causing her disgrace in the eyes of Society, and she's sent to her sister's home. It is hoped that her influence will make her behave like a dutiful daughter . . . but the rebellious Lucy has other ideas.

THE ABANDONED RAKE

Emily Harland

When Joanna Winterton's fiance is killed, she finds it difficult to mourn him, for she only had scant admiration for the little she knew of him. Relieved to be free of such an odious commitment and certainly not desirous of the spurious sympathy of society, she retreats to the Lake District. Meanwhile, Sir Lucas Montfort flees to the Lakes to heal his wounded pride after he is left waiting — quite abandoned — at the altar. When he crosses paths with Joanna in Grasmere, neither party is pleased . . . but the reluctant pair soon find that they have more in common than they think . . .